Flint

Book 4:

RESURRECTION

Flint

Book 4:

RESURRECTION

Treasure Hernandez

www.urbanbooks.net

Urban Books, LLC
78 East Industry Court
Deer Park, NY 11729

Flint Book 4: Resurrection Copyright © 2008 Treasure
Hernandez

ISBN 13: 978-1-60162-442-0
ISBN 10: 1-60162-442-5

First Mass Market Printing March 2011
First Trade Paperback Printing December 2008
Printed in the United States of America

10   9   8   7   6   5   4   3   2   1

*This is a work of fiction. Any references or similarities to ac-
tual events, real people, living, or dead, or to real locales are
intended to give the novel a sense of reality. Any similarity in
other names, characters, places, and incidents is entirely coin-
cidental.*

Distributed by Kensington Publishing Corp.
Submit Wholesale Orders to:
Kensington Publishing Corp.
C/O Penguin Group (USA) Inc.
Attention: Order Processing
405 Murray Hill Parkway
East Rutherford, NJ 07073-2316
Phone: 1-800-526-0275
Fax: 1-800-227-9604

ACKNOWLEDGMENTS

First and foremost, I would like to thank God for all the blessings he has bestowed upon me.

I would like to thank all my fans in Flint who knew where I was coming from. Thanks for all your support.

Please send all letters to Urban Books. They will make sure I get them.

Holla at your girl!!!!

Treasure Hernandez
c/o Urban Books
1199 Straight Path
West Babylon, NY 11704

Love & Peace,
Treasure

Prologue

Mimi watched as Malek clumsily stumbled onto the motel bed and lay flat on his back. He gripped his rock-hard dick and Mimi almost felt sorry for him. She knew that Maury would kill him after he got him to take him to his stash spot, but greed pushed her to let the scene unfold. She seductively walked over to Malek and dropped to her knees. She then began to unbutton his Evisu jeans as he tried to pull away.

"What you doing, ma?" he said almost incoherently, slurring each syllable.

"Just relax, Malek. Your mouth is saying no, but your friend down here is saying yes," Mimi said just before she took Malek's ten inches into her mouth. She had purposely left the door unlocked so Maury could creep in. *Where this nigga at? He's taking all day,* she thought as she continued to go up and down on Malek's shaft then began playing with the tip of it with her tongue.

She paused to look at Malek, and as she looked up, what she saw scared the living shit out of her. No longer looking distraught and confused like he was moments before, Malek was smiling with his pistol in his hand, his demeanor totally changed.

"You look surprised," Malek said just before he struck her in the temple, causing her to fly onto the carpeted floor of the motel.

She gripped her bloody forehead in agony, and her vision became temporarily blurred.

"You thought I didn't see you try to slip me that spiked drink, ma? Huh? I ain't new to this, I'm true to this!" Malek yelled as he stood up and put his pipe back in his jeans.

Only moments before, he'd pretended to drink the spiked liquor, but had quickly poured it on the floor when Mimi's head was turned.

"Now look at you!" he said, his gun pointed at Mimi. "That's why niggas can't trust these hoes out here! I know a nigga is about to come in here any second now. I saw yo' dumb ass leave the door unlocked, and I peeped you scoping out that blue car that followed us in here."

"Malek, wait! I—"

Malek struck her again in the head with the butt of the gun. Then he aimed the gun at her head once again. "Who is trying to hurt Halleigh? Were you telling the truth?"

Mimi, scared to lie, tried to tell the truth. "No, it was a—"

Before Mimi could get out her sentence, Malek

sent a hollow-tip through her chest with his si-
lenced pistol. He'd heard all he needed to hear.
To his surprise, he wasn't even afraid of catching
his second body, the rage inside of him making it
easier to pull the trigger. Now his only concern was
the guy who was scheduled to come in the room at
any second.

Halleigh couldn't wipe the smile off her face if
she wanted to. She was so happy about Malek's
proposition, she couldn't wait to move forward
and leave her current lifestyle in the dust. She
rummaged through her clothes, trying to stuff all
she could into her luggage. Malek had made her
feel like a new woman, and she was about to start
her life with him.

It only took her thirty minutes to pack up everything. When she called Malek's cell and he didn't
pick up, she left a message that she was ready and
wanted to know where he could pick her up. She
then sat on the porch waiting for her Prince
Charming to arrive. *Hurry up and get here, Malek,*
she said to herself as she anxiously waited.

Malek stood over Maury's shaking body as he
watched him struggle for his life. Malek had
caught him with four slugs to the chest right at the
moment he walked through the motel door. Malek
held the smoking gun in his hand and began to

tremble slightly. In his twenty years on earth, he had never killed anyone, but now in the past couple of weeks, he had caught three bodies.

Malek witnessed Maury take his last breath and then quickly fled the scene. He ran over to the club to put Joe on to what had happened.

For all Malek knew, Sweets had set this whole thing up in an attempt to take him out. On the other hand, it could have just been Mimi trying to set him up on her own. But, either way it went, he needed to confide in his mentor. If Sweets was setting Malek up for the okey-doke, then nine times out of ten, he was setting Joe up too, so Malek felt like he had to warn him.

Malek's heart raced frantically as he approached the back entrance of the club. He noticed the large group of people running out of the club in a frenzy. Then he soon found out why. He heard the gunfire coming from the club and quickly gripped his pistol tighter and ran to the back entrance, where he knew Joe would be coming out. He spotted Joe's car, and then he saw Joe and the young lady he was with earlier jump into it.

"Joe!" Malek yelled as he ran to the truck.

"Come on, Malek. Jump in!" Joe screamed as he waved Malek over.

The girl took the backseat, and Malek jumped into the passenger side.

"Joe," Malek said, nearly out of breath, "a nigga tried to set me up in the—"

Before he could finish, the girl reached into her garter belt and pulled out a snub-nosed .22 pistol.

She let off a shot to the back of Joe's head and then reached over and shot Malek three times to the chest. Joe's limp head rested on his horn, causing it to honk continuously, blood covering the front window.

The girl that Sweets sent for the job smiled. She loved what she did, because she was damn good at it. She was one of the most prolific hit-hoes (as in hitman) in the underground world. She could get to dons quicker than anyone could even fathom. She looked at Malek as he took his last breath and closed his eyes.

Just as she was about to step out of the car to meet Sweets in the front as he had instructed her earlier, a phone rang. It was Malek's cell.

"Hello?" the mystery woman said, trying to add salt to the wound. She always did menacing things like that. She got an adrenaline rush and laughter out of her bold, sinister humor.

"Who is this? Where is Malek?" the female voice on the other end of the phone asked.

"He's sleeping," she said, before letting out a big laugh and hanging up. She left the car, leaving Joe and Malek slumped.

After fifteen minutes of waiting on Malek to pick her up, Halleigh tried calling him on his cell phone again, but when a woman picked up and told her that he was sleeping, she was dumbfounded. She just looked at her phone in disbelief. Her heart crumbled at the fact that another

woman had picked up Malek's phone. He was supposed to be on his way to pick her up, yet he was
with another woman.

I knew it was too good to be true. I knew it. Tears
began to flow down her cheeks. Once again, her
heart had been broken in two.

Chapter One

Malek woke up with an aching pain in his chest. He looked over to his left and saw his mentor, Jamaica Joe, slumped on the steering wheel. It all happened so fast that Malek couldn't believe it.

"Joe," Malek whispered. He tried to shake him, but it was to no avail; Joe was already gone. The bullet-proof vest that Malek was wearing protected him from the bullets that the mysterious woman had shot at him moments before, but there was still a nagging pain in his shoulder that wouldn't go away.

"Joe!" Malek managed to scream as he continued to shake him. He couldn't grasp the reality. Shock took over his reactions as he tried his hardest to wake Jamaica Joe. Blood trickled onto Malek's hand. That's when he noticed the small hole in the back of Jamaica Joe's head.

Seeing his big brother, mentor, and teacher gone was too much to bear. Malek let out a painful roar as tears welled up in his eyes, and his vision began to blur. Malek heard the sound of sirens as he looked in the rearview mirror.

As he reached for the door, an intense pain shot through his body. "Aghh shit!" he yelled out. He stumbled out of the car, and for the first time he noticed all of the blood on his own shirt. He patted his body frantically to see where he was hit. He was in shock and couldn't pinpoint where the pain in his body was coming from.

An ambulance and police cars pulled up simultaneously as Malek fell to his knees.

"Put your hands up where I can see them!" the police called.

"It ain't me! They got Joe! Joe in the car," he muttered as held his body up by placing one hand on the ground. "Help Joe!" he shouted as he began to cough up blood. The paramedics rushed over to him and immediately began work.

"We have a bullet wound to the shoulder. Get me some oxygen and let's start him on an IV," the medic called out to his peers.

Malek felt weak, and the taste of blood in his mouth frightened him.

"We're going to have to question him," one of the officers stated.

"You're going to have to wait until after he gets this bullet removed. If not, he's going to bleed to death," the medic stated sternly as he helped place Malek's body on a stretcher. Malek was slipping in and out of consciousness and was losing pints of blood at a time.

As Malek's head fell to the side, his eyes witnessed the police zip up Jamaica Joe's body bag. "Joe," he whispered faintly.

Anger ripped through Malek. Joe had been so close to his departure from the dope game. He had taken careful steps, crossing every *T* and dotting every *I*, to ensure that he made it out of the game alive and free. Unfortunately someone had other plans for him. On the night of his farewell party to the dope game, he said farewell to his life.

Malek knew that there was only one person who would be so bold to attempt a hit on Jamaica Joe. He knew exactly who was behind this hit, and vowed to make Sweets pay if he lived to see another day.

Halleigh sat by the window, staring blankly at the darkened city block, her heart aching at the fact that Malek was with another girl. But she couldn't help it. She didn't care if he had a thousand other girls besides her; she had to be a part of his life.

Her heart beat rapidly as she impatiently waited for Malek to show up at her door. She was furious with him, but she needed him. She was so close to having him. *Where is he?* she thought solemnly as tears fell from her face. Her anxiety was eating her up inside. Every time a car rode down her block, she would go to the door and hope that it was

Malek pulling up to get her. She thought it was Malek every time a headlight shone through her window. Every rumble of an engine could've been him.

"Why isn't he here?" she asked aloud. "He's probably fucking with some bitch." She checked the clock on the wall and noticed that it read 4:40 A.M. *He was supposed to be here three hours ago.* Her mind was telling her to give up hope, but her heart wouldn't allow her to.

Halleigh sat in front of the window until dusk turned to dawn, and the nightlife gave way to the bright sunlight, signifying the start of another day. "He's not coming," she uttered as she finally came to terms with her reality. She had hoped that things would go back to normal and that Malek could look past all of the things that she'd done since she'd last seen him, but with daylight came the realization that things could never go back to the way they used to be. Too much had happened. She had changed in the most drastic way.

"He doesn't want me anymore," she cried as she dropped to the floor next to her packed bags. Tears fell freely. She didn't blame him for not showing up, since she wasn't the same girl that he'd once cherished. She had turned too many tricks, taken too many drugs, acquired too many demons. She was definitely not the innocent teenage girl that he had known.

At nineteen, she had been through more than the average forty-year-old, and the mental and physical abuse that she had encountered over the past two years of her life had left her confused. She had been pimped, turned out, and left for dead.

"Why would he want me?" she asked herself.

Ring! Ring!

The screeching blare of the telephone startled her, and she staggered to her feet to answer it. She silently wished it to be Malek. She wiped her eyes and nose as she tried to calm down before picking up the phone.

"Hello?" she stated, her voice cracking in her attempt to sound okay.

"Halleigh! Oh my God, Halleigh, Maury got shot tonight! He's at Hurley Hospital. The doctors won't tell me anything!" Tasha screamed.

"What?" Halleigh responded in shock.

"Halleigh, just please come down here," Tasha pleaded. "I can't handle this by myself. He's all I've got."

The line went dead before Halleigh could reply, but she knew that she had to put her feelings aside so that she could be there for Tasha. Tasha had been the only person to stand by her side through her ups and downs, and she felt obligated to return the favor. She grabbed her coat without hesitation and rushed out the door.

Tasha stood in front of the nurse's desk, impatiently waiting to receive news on her brother's condition. "Is he okay?" When she didn't get an immediate response, she yelled in frustration, "Why won't you tell me anything?"

"You really should wait for the doctor," the nurse told her. "He will help you understand what happened."

"Fuck you mean?" Tasha stated in exasperation. "Understand what? What happened? Please just tell me that Maury is okay."

"I'm sorry, miss, I can't," the nurse replied.

Tasha knocked all of the nurse's papers off the counter and stormed out of the hospital in a pained rage. Her head felt like it would explode. *I need to get some fresh air,* she thought as she rushed out of the double doors that led to the emergency room parking lot.

Just as Tasha was about to sit down on the curb, she saw Halleigh running toward her. She stood and hugged her tightly.

"What happened, Tash? Where is he?" Halleigh asked with concern as Tasha sobbed in her arms. Halleigh didn't know what to do. She had never seen Tasha like this. Tasha was the foundation of their friendship. She was the strong one. The leader. The roles had quickly reversed, and now Halleigh was the one trying to figure things out.

"I don't know, Hal. They ain't telling me shit. This is bad, Hal." Then she added in a whisper, "We should've just stayed in New York. If we had, he wouldn't be lying up in this hospital."

Halleigh knew that she couldn't cry. She had to be strong for her friend, but on the inside she prayed that Maury was okay. Halleigh and Maury had a relationship that only the two of them could understand. He'd made Halleigh feel worthy of love, always standing beside her, encouraging her to forget her past and live for the future. Halleigh couldn't really explain her strong feelings for Maury, but to her it was one of those love-at-first-sight kind of things.

Halleigh had met Maury when she, Tasha, and Mimi decided to head to New York and sort things out after the three of them had set up their pimp, Manolo, to be robbed and arrested. The three of them were in on the robbery and had decided to come to New York, where they hooked up with Tasha's brother Maury. He helped them move the bricks that they had received as part of Manolo's setup and robbery.

After a long drive from Flint, Michigan to Brooklyn, New York, Halleigh, Tasha, and Mimi let themselves into Maury's home because he wasn't at home when they'd arrived. Halleigh was mad tired and had fallen asleep as soon as they made themselves comfortable in Maury's house. She eventually awoke and decided to take a shower. At the time she woke, Maury still wasn't home, and Tasha and Mimi had gone out to get something to eat. So when Maury finally arrived home, he was shocked to find a naked woman in his shower.

Halleigh smiled on the inside as she stood with Tasha, memories of the day she'd met Maury replaying in her mind.

"Fuck is you?" Maury barked as he pulled back his shower curtain and saw a screaming Halleigh trying to cover up her body.

"Do you fuckin' mind?" Halleigh screamed back at

Maury as she stepped out of the shower and searched for something to put on. "Get out!" she yelled.

"This is my crib!" Maury said bluntly as he looked at Halleigh's body. "Here, cover yourself up, shorty."

Halleigh snatched the towel from Maury and quickly wrapped it tightly around her body.

"Now do you want to tell me who the hell you are and what you're doing in my house?"

Maury had calmed down his tone, and Halleigh could see that he was purposely trying to be gentle with her.

And from that moment on, Maury had always acted graciously and gently with Halleigh, making her feel safe and secure just from his presence, which was non-menacing, unlike the horrible men she'd had in her life.

Maury's gentleness made Halleigh open up to him and tell him things about her past that she was highly ashamed of. Yet, that just seemed to draw him even closer to her.

If she wasn't so hung up on Malek, she could've easily seen herself falling for Maury, but her feelings for Malek were too strong for her to let go. Malek was a part of her, and she couldn't let her heart love another if she tried.

"Everything's gon' be all right," Halleigh said unconvincingly. "Come on, it's too cold to be standing out here. Let's wait inside."

Halleigh and Tasha made their way back to the waiting room, where they both sat solemnly in silence, consumed with their own thoughts.

It was now almost noon. Ten hours had passed

since Maury had been shot. Tasha had been in the hospital now for about three hours, yet she was still in the dark about her brother's status. She was more than thankful that Maury had her name listed under *Sister* in the address portion of his BlackBerry. That was the only way that the doctors were able to contact her to inform her that her brother had been shot. But now the unending wait to find out his condition was like torture.

Another hour passed before a doctor finally came out to see them.

"How is my brother?" Tasha asked as soon as she saw the doctor step into the room.

"I apologize for keeping you waiting this long," the doctor stated. "I don't know how to tell you this, but your brother was D.O.A. We called you down here because we needed a relative to identify his body."

Halleigh watched as Tasha broke down.

Tasha's body went numb as she looked at the man through glassy eyes. "D.O.A.? Identify his— No!" she cried. "No! God, no!"

"I'm sorry for your loss," the doctor stated out of routine. His tone held no sympathy, and he barely looked at Tasha as he delivered the worst news she'd ever received. "I'll give you a few minutes to cope with the information I've given you. I will still need you to ID the body." He walked out of the room without once looking back.

Tasha's screams could be heard through the entire emergency room. Tears fell from Halleigh's eyes as she wrapped her arms around her friend.

Tasha clung to Halleigh, and the two girls sat down, rocking each other back and forth in an attempt to deal with their grief. Although Halleigh's pain wasn't as great, she was still hurt by Maury's death. He had treated her like she was worth more than gold, and she appreciated his brief presence in her life.

God, please take care of him. Halleigh looked toward the sky as she held onto Tasha, but let go when she looked up and saw the news flash across the waiting room TV. Malek's picture was on the morning news.

"Turn that up!" Halleigh yelled as she jumped up, leaving Tasha's side and rushing to the nurse's station. "Please turn that up!" she repeated. The nurse increased the volume on the TV, and Halleigh watched in desperation.

"Hi, this is Grace Stocker reporting live from Celebrations nightclub in Flint, Michigan. Last night this was the scene of a deadly shooting. Two people were shot and killed. One was injured. These deaths bring the total to thirty-seven in Flint's murder count, making it one of the most violent cities per capita in America."

Halleigh shook her head in disbelief. "He didn't show up last night. He was shot," she whispered. "He was dying."

As Malek's picture was displayed on the screen again, the newscaster continued, "Malek Johnson was among those individuals involved in the chaos. Two years ago he had been deemed Flint's star and was expected to be the number one draft pick in the NBA. Now he is involved in yet another violent encounter.

"Viewers may remember the violence and chaos that erupted at Berston Park during a basketball game between rival drug dealers that turned deadly. Malek Johnson was shot at that event, and now here we have yet another incident where Malek Johnson has been shot. Just another indication of how bad things are in the city of Flint."

Halleigh tuned the reporter out and rushed back to the nurse's station. "Is Malek Johnson here?" she asked, knowing there was a good chance that he could be in the hospital somewhere. "Please tell me he's here."

The nurse typed in Malek's name and nodded her head. "Malek Johnson is in room eight-fourteen."

Halleigh looked back toward Tasha, who was still grieving uncontrollably over the loss of her brother. She ran over to her and kneeled by her side. "I'll be back, Tasha. I have to go check on Malek. He could be lying up in here dead and I wouldn't even know it. Are you going to be okay?"

Tasha nodded her head.

Halleigh rushed to the nearest elevator in search of Malek. She stepped inside and closed her eyes as she prepared herself for what she was about to see. *Please, God, let him be okay.*

Malek, grateful that he was still alive, considered himself lucky to be breathing as he lay on the hospital bed. Something told him to put on his bullet-proof vest the night of Joe's party, and he was glad that he had followed his instincts. His vest was the only thing that saved him from certain death. One of the bullets had struck him in the shoulder, but most of them hit his vest, leaving him with some bad bruises and one gunshot wound. But he would rather have bruises and a bad shoulder than holes any day.

Having seen Jamaica Joe get shot in the head, he couldn't help but feel that he had cheated death. The emotions that he felt for his man were overwhelming. Jamaica Joe had been the one person who had reached out to him after his NBA scandal. Even after the murder of Malek's mother, Jamaica Joe supported him like only family could. Jamaica Joe had become Malek's family, and now Malek had been forced to watch him die.

The doctors had given him Vicodin to take some of his pain away, and the potent prescription drug had him woozy. He could barely keep his eyes open, but he was paranoid that someone wanted him dead, so he made an effort to stay awake. He also knew that the police would have some questions for him. They would want to know how he had acquired a bullet-proof vest, but he wasn't going to stick around and wait for them to question him.

Malek focused his attention on the door as Halleigh walked into the room. The room was dark, but he still recognized her. He could tell by the way that she walked that it was her. Her steps were timid, and she was afraid of the condition that Malek could be in.

"They got Joe, Halleigh. She blew his brains out right in front of me," he stated without looking up in her direction.

"Oh my God, thank you," she whispered as she walked to his bedside and kissed his cheek. Her mind wasn't on Jamaica Joe. She was just happy to see that Malek hadn't joined him in death. She sobbed as she kissed his face over and over again.

Tears from her face dripped onto his skin, and he reached out for her hand. "Why you crying, ma?" he asked.

"I don't know. I'm just glad you're okay. When you didn't show up, I thought . . ." She couldn't finish her sentence.

"I'm right here, Hal. I told you I ain't goin' nowhere. It's me and you against the world," he whispered as he traced her face with his fingertips. "Okay?"

She nodded her head with understanding.

"Now help me out of this bed," he stated. "I got to get up out of here before the police come through."

As Halleigh helped him out of the bed, he grimaced. She was careful not to touch his bandaged chest.

"Are you sure you're okay to leave?" she asked.

"Yeah, I'm good. I was wearing a vest, so the shots to the chest didn't penetrate. I took one in the shoulder, though, and my entire arm hurts like shit," he answered.

Malek reached for Halleigh, and she helped him stand by putting one arm behind his back as he draped his good arm across her shoulder. "Everything's gon' be good, Hal. I promise you, I'ma take care of you."

"But what about you? You just got shot. Who did this to you?" Halleigh stopped to look into Malek's eyes.

Malek sighed as he felt the throbbing in his chest. He grabbed the back of Halleigh's neck and brought her close as he kissed her on the lips. "Do you trust me?" he asked.

She nodded her head.

"Let me hear you say it."

"I trust you, Malek."

"All right then. Let me be your man and take care of you. You don't need to worry about anything."

Halleigh smiled slightly because she was finally where she wanted to be—with Malek.

Reminiscent of when the rapper Tupac Shakur had been ambushed and shot in New York City and then immediately checked himself out of the hospital against his doctors' wishes, Malek, fearing that his life was still in jeopardy, decided to "pull a Tupac Shakur," and checked himself out against medical advice.

Halleigh held onto Malek and helped him into a wheelchair and then wheeled him out of the hospital without ever looking back. They were about to begin a new life together, with Malek as the boss and Halleigh as his wifey.

Tasha stepped into the cold room and stared at the bodies lying on the steel tables and covered with white sheets. Her heart felt as if it would explode from fear. Deep within she knew that her brother was lying lifeless on top of one of the tables.

The coroner looked at the disheveled woman before him, and pity filled her face. A police detective stood in the corner of the room and watched her every move as the coroner led her to one of the bodies.

"Are you ready?" the woman asked as she put her hands on the white sheet.

Tasha wanted to respond, but the huge lump in her throat stopped her from speaking.

After a couple seconds, the coroner pulled the covers back, revealing Maury. Tasha's hand flew to her mouth as she doubled over in grief. "Maury! God, no! No!" she cried as she caressed her deceased brother's face. His skin was cold and held a blue hue. The four bullet holes in his chest were red, and dried-up blood had crusted around the wounds. The coroner nodded toward the detective, who then walked toward Tasha.

"Miss, when your brother was killed, he wasn't alone. We have another victim, a female, and we can't seem to find anyone that knows her. Would you mind taking a look to see if you recognize her?" the detective asked. He didn't even wait for her to agree before leading her over to another steel table.

The coroner followed and then pulled the sheet back.

"Mimi?" Tasha whispered. "Mimi!" Tasha couldn't stop the vomit that came up. She threw up all over the floor. The murder of her brother and her close friend was too much for her to bear. "Why would someone do this?" she asked as she glanced back toward her brother.

"I can't do this," she stated before racing out of the room. She could hear her heart pounding in her head, and her breathing became erratic and shallow. She couldn't breathe, and her stomach was twisted in knots. *Maury's gone, Mimi's dead. What were they doing together? Who did this?* She couldn't contain her emotions. She didn't even make it down the hallway before she passed out on the hospital floor.

When she came to, she was in no position to deal with detectives, but at the same time, she had to pull herself together because she wanted to help the police find the people who had done this to two of the people that she was closest to in this world.

"Tasha, we had several uniformed police officers taking statements after the violence erupted at Celebrations nightclub. And although Mimi and your brother were not killed at the nightclub, when we found out about their murders, we were able to go and re-interview some of the people who had given statements to the uniformed officers. At least three people have verified that they saw Malek Johnson leaving Celebrations with Mimi. So, before we question Mr. Johnson, we want to know from you if know Malek Johnson."

Tahsa's heartbeat immediately picked up, and while she ignored the cop's question, she wracked her brain, trying to think back to everything that had transpired the night before. And before she knew it, a light bulb went off in her head, and she could see the whole layout of the VIP area. Yes, she definitely remembered seeing Malek and Mimi talking.

What the fuck?

"Tasha, I know this is difficult, but if there is anything you can think of, it will probably help, no matter how small of a detail you may think it is."

"Malek? Yeah, who in Flint doesn't know Malek Johnson? He was damn near the LeBron James of Flint."

"Did you happen to see him with Mimi at Celebrations?"

Tasha paused; then she looked at the detective and shook her head. "Nah, to be honest, I seen Malek that night, but I never saw him with Mimi," Tasha lied. She didn't know what angle the cops were coming from, but she was street-smart enough to know to keep her fucking mouth shut, especially when it came to talking to "Jake."

Something the fuck ain't right! Tasha thought, but

she just couldn't figure out what it was. She knew that she had to speak to both Halleigh and Malek to see if she could make sense out of Malek's name being in the police's mouth. She knew that if they had suspicions about Malek having something to do with Mimi's murder, then they also had to have suspicions about him being in on Maury's murder.

What the fuck? Tasha couldn't help but notice how things seemed like they were quickly going from bad to worse.

Chapter Two

After she helped Malek into the backseat of the cab, Halleigh turned back toward the hospital.

Malek could see her hesitation. "What we waiting on, Hal? Let's get out of here." Malek held out his hand for her.

"Tasha is in there, Malek. Her brother was killed last night. I have to go check on her," Halleigh stated. "Just wait five minutes for me."

Malek shook his head and replied, "Nah, ma, you've got to leave that life alone. All those chicks you were rolling with are dead to you now. I don't want you around anything or anyone that links you to that nigga Manolo, understand?"

"But, Malek, she's my friend and she needs me," Halleigh pleaded as she looked back at the hospital doors.

"So do I, Hal. I need you, and you can't have both worlds. You either with me, or you not. If you choose me, all that Manolo Mami shit and all the drugs you was fucking with got to be a thing of the past."

Halleigh looked back one last time at the hospital and then got into the cab with Malek. Her heart ached as the cab pulled away from the hospital. Malek was putting her between a rock and a hard place. Tasha was her closest friend, and now she was abandoning her.

She needs me, Hal thought as a tear slid down her face.

Malek quickly wiped it away. "This is a new beginning, Hal," he whispered as he pulled her head near and kissed the side of her face.

Halleigh gave him a weak smile as she reached out for his hand and intertwined her fingers with his. The warmth that generated between them was something that she'd been wanting to feel for the past two years, and now that she had found her way back to him, she was never letting go. She told herself that she had to sacrifice her friendship with Tasha in order to save her relationship with Malek.

He's worth it, she thought.

Against Malek's better judgment, they pulled up to his one-bedroom apartment, and she helped him out of the cab and up the steps to the third floor. Malek didn't let Halleigh know it, but he was feeling a bit paranoid. He wanted to avoid his South Side enemies, and at the same time, he wanted to avoid any questions from the police, so he knew that going to his crib wasn't the best idea.

But in the condition that he was in, he really wanted to avoid moving around too much.

When they entered the apartment, Halleigh helped him to the bedroom and sat him down on the edge of the bed. Malek looked up at her, and for the first time, he noticed a change in her, a sexy matureness. She seemed to have lost her girl-hood innocence in a way that made her look and come across more mature, more sexy.

"You look good, Hal," he commented.

The two years that they had been separated had matured her, but they had also hardened her. She put her head down as she thought of all that she'd been through.

Malek immediately noticed her embarrassment, but didn't comment on it. He didn't want to make her feel worse than she already did. He was aware that she would have to rebuild her self-confidence. He only hoped that she would eventually be the same girl that he had known before her life was turned upside down.

Malek pulled her down onto the bed and she lay directly underneath him. The smell of her was intoxicating, and for the first time in two years, he felt whole. Halleigh was the missing piece to his life puzzle, and now that she was back, he was determined to never let her go.

"Hold up," he said as he eased out of the bed and went into a safe in his closet. He pulled out a .45 automatic and went to make sure that his apartment door was locked. After taking shots to

the chest, he was paranoid. He knew that somebody wanted him dead and that he had to be on
point until he got to the bottom of it.

He went back to the room, lay down next to Hal,
and put the handgun beside his pillow as a precaution.

Hal snuggled closed to him, and he held her in
his arms. It hurt like hell, but in spite of the physical pain he was feeling, he had to hold Halleigh
just to have her close to him. The silence between
them was a comfortable one, and eventually it
transformed into the first comfortable sleep that
either of them had experienced in more than two
years.

The next morning Malek awoke to excruciating
pain shooting up and down the left side of his
body. He knew that his arm would hurt, but he
had no idea how badly. He was careful not to dis-
turb Halleigh as he got out of bed and made his
way to the bathroom. He opened the medicine
cabinet and retrieved some Tylenol. Taking five at
a time, he hoped that the mild over-the-counter
drug would relieve his pain.

His thoughts drifted to Jamaica Joe, and he
gripped the sink in agony over the thought of losing his mentor. Now it was his time to step up to the
plate, but it didn't feel right without Jamaica Joe by
his side. Jamaica Joe had ensured that he'd learned
all that he needed to know regarding the streets,
but Malek knew that he had some big shoes to fill.

At twenty, he was in a position to be the king of the streets. The North Side belonged to him. He had managed to save $50,000 while hustling under Joe. It wasn't much, but it was more than the average hustler had in Flint.

He needed to come up with a plan. He already had the connect. Joe had made sure that he was in line with a supreme coke supplier, so that wasn't an issue. The problem was Fredro didn't deal in small quantities. He supplied Jamaica Joe kilos in bulk, and Malek's money wasn't long enough to cop the usual twenty-five ki's. Fredro was giving up the goods for ten stacks a ki, but that price came along with the agreement that he would buy the same amount each time. Malek needed $200,000 more to make the deal happen, which meant he had to flip and re-flip his money in order to fuck with Fredro.

Malek looked in his bathroom mirror and saw Halleigh enter the room. She walked up behind him and wrapped her arms around his body, resting her face on his toned upper back.

"Hey, you," she greeted with a sincere smile. "How you feel?"

"I'm good," he replied as he turned around and kissed her on the forehead. "Just thinking about everything. I just can't believe I'm about to bury my man in a few days. That shit is fucking with me, Hal. You don't know. Joe been like family since the first day we met. I should've talked him out of throwing that party. He would still be here if I had been smarter."

"I didn't know Jamaica Joe that well, but I'm sorry that his death is hurting you, Malek. I do know that his death ain't on you, though. You can't control anybody else's destiny. If you could, none of this would've ever happened to us.

"I just want you to be okay. I want us to be how we were before all this bullshit sent us in different directions," she said. "Do you think we'll ever get back everything that we lost? I mean, time is something that you can't make up for. Two years have passed us by. We haven't spoken or touched one another.

"I'm not the same person that I was at seventeen. Do you think you can learn to love the new me?"

Halleigh was right. She didn't know Jamaica Joe that well, definitely not the way Malek knew him. Malek knew that he would've been sitting in the jail cell probably doing football numbers, if it weren't for Jamaica Joe, who, out of the kindness of his heart when he didn't even know Malek, had his own lawyer defend Malek on the stickup that he had ended up catching a case for.

Malek also knew that Jamaica Joe had validated him when he put him on making him a major player in the drug game almost overnight. Yup, Malek knew that he would've been broke, forgotten about, in jail, and always referred to as the dumb muthafucka who fucked up his shot at NBA riches.

"I don't have to learn to love you, Hal. You a part of me, so I can never stop caring for you. We've got some issues that we need to work through, but we gon' be all right. I'ma make sure of that. I'm not the same person either. We all grow. Whether we grow for the good or bad is up to us. I'm about to be the king of this shit, believe that. All you gon' have to worry about is making your man look good, a'ight. Stand by your man and everything will be good for us."

Malek went into his room and into his safe. He pulled out two rubber-banded stacks of money and tossed them to Halleigh. "Go buy yourself some new gear. I don't want you in nothing some other nigga bought for you. Make sure you get a dress to wear to Joe's funeral."

Halleigh accepted the money. She had no desire to go to Jamaica Joe's funeral, but she knew that she had to go. Halleigh knew that the average person would never understand what it was like to not want to go to certain events out of fear constantly wondering if you were gonna run into someone who had paid to fuck you. That was the main reason she didn't want to go to the funeral. But she also knew that Malek expected her to go, and she didn't want to disappoint him.

She wanted to be at Maury's funeral to pay her respects and be there for her girl, but she knew Malek would never allow it. She had been down with the South Side for so long, it was going to be hard for her to adjust her loyalty. She was never loyal to Manolo or Sweets, but her girls were all she had, and she had grown to love them both. They had been her sisters. Just like Malek was connected to Joe, she was connected to them. Mimi and Tasha were the ones who'd helped her make it through their pimp's controlling and viciously abusive ways. They had also helped her make it through her drug addiction, which she had used as an escape from the emotional bondage that prostitution had held her in.

More importantly, they had helped her and helped themselves literally escape from the clutches of Manolo, their pimp. Now they were off-limits to her, and she couldn't help but feel like a traitor. She at least wanted to say good-bye to her girls.

"Malek, I know you don't want me to be around Tasha or Mimi, but I really need to go back and get some of my things. I don't need to bring my old clothes, but there are some personal items that I'd like to keep," she stated.

Malek looked at her skeptically.

"I promise it will be quick. I just need to pick up a few things," she said, trying to reassure him.

Malek agreed, and an hour later, he was driving her out to the suburbs of Flint to the apartment that she'd shared with her friends.

When Malek pulled up to the apartment complex, Halleigh saw that Tasha's car was parked in her normal spot. She looked over at Malek and said, "I'll be right back."

"Take your time and make sure you have everything you need. There's no coming back here after today," he stated seriously.

Halleigh nodded and took a deep breath as she exited the car and entered the building.

She used her key to enter the apartment. It was silent inside as she made her way back to Tasha's room. She knocked lightly before entering. "Tash," she called out.

Tasha didn't respond. Her back was toward Halleigh, and she was curled up in a fetal position on her bed. Her hair was all over her head, and she stared blankly at the wall in front of her.

Halleigh walked over to her bed, sat on the edge of it, and stroked Tasha's hair lightly. "Tash, I've got to talk to you about something, and I don't have a lot of—"

"She's dead too," Tasha interrupted.

"What? Who?" Hal asked in confusion.

"Mimi's dead," she stated through her cries. "She was with Maury when he got killed."

Halleigh's mouth dropped open. She whispered, "No, Tasha, please tell me you're lying."

Tasha didn't respond.

"Tasha! Please!" she begged, hoping that the news wasn't true.

"Halleigh, she's gone! They're both gone!" Tasha stated. "We're all we got."

Those words made Halleigh feel ten times worse than she already did. Tasha needed her, yet Halleigh was here to tell her that she was letting go of everything and everyone that reminded her of her past.

"Tash, we need to talk," she began. She tried to swallow the lump in her throat, but it wasn't going away. "I can't stay here, Tash. I have to move on with my life, Tasha. Malek doesn't want me to—"

"Malek? Hal, my brother and our friend were just killed. I have been here for you since the day I met you. You mean to tell me, just because you back with that nigga, you gon' act like I don't exist? You are like my sister." Tasha stood up from her bed.

"Tasha, it's not like that! I love you. You're my girl. I just can't afford to lose Malek again."

"The world doesn't revolve around Malek, Halleigh!"

"My world does! I met you in a whorehouse. You were the madame that was supposed to help my pimp keep me in line! Malek doesn't understand how you helped me. He doesn't want me around anybody that is down with the South Side. I have to respect it, Tasha. He's my man, and I love him."

"So fuck me and everybody who gave a damn about you when he left you for dead?" Tasha yelled, with one hand on her hip as she stared incredulously at her friend. "Fuck me, fuck Mimi. Fuck Maury too, Halleigh? My brother loved you. I've never seen him look at a chick the way he looked at you. Fuck him, though. Fuck that he came here to look after your skinny ass!"

"That's not fair, Tash!"

"No, you're not fair, Hal! And you know what else? I been sitting up here trying with everything I had to block some shit out, saying to myself, 'Nah, there's no way that Halleigh could do me like that.' But I guess I was wrong! Your nose is so far up Malek's ass that it doesn't even bother you that he murdered Maury and Mimi! Right, bitch?

Tell me I'm lying and I swear on everything, I'll lay your ass out right here!"

Halleigh felt the tears coming to her eyes. "Tasha, what are you talking about?" Halleigh asked, a twisted and confused look on her face.

"Halleigh, stop with the bullshit. You know what I'm saying is true, and that's why you ain't been around and that's why you running off! The cops told me what was up, and I played shit cool and covered for Malek's ass. Why? Because that's how I do for my people! And because I never in my wildest thoughts would have believed that Malek would do some shit like this!"

Halleigh burst out into tears.

"Halleigh, enough of the crocodile tears and all that fake shit!"

"Fake? Tasha, this ain't fake! You . . . I . . . I mean, I know you are hurting and going through it, but you're talking crazy. And I'm dealing with a lot of conflicting shit too, and I don't even know what is going on."

"Halleigh, you wanna know what's the fuck is going on? Yeah, whatever! But I tell you what; you walk outta here, and I'll know what was up and what went down, and you won't have to say shit. And if you stay, then I'll be on my knees apologizing and forever grateful. But understand this: if you leave after all I done did for you, then it's on! On the life of my brother and on the life of Mimi, it's on!"

Halleigh was feeling beyond stressed out. She shook her head and stared at Tasha. Then she left the room and went into the one that she had once occupied. All of her things were as she had left them. She grabbed a small laundry basket and placed some of her items inside, including a few of the pieces that Maury had purchased for her while she was in New York.

She wouldn't tell Malek why they were important to her, but she had to have them. Maury had helped her rebuild her self-esteem in a way that Malek couldn't. See, she looked at Maury as a neutral person who didn't judge her or come down on her, and in the process, he helped to validate her. She was eternally grateful to him for that. With Malek, he didn't judge her or come down on her for anything, but he was someone that she'd loved and known and had history with. So, in her mind, she never really knew if Malek's actions toward her were stemming from a genuine place in his heart or out of pity for her.

More tears came to her eyes when she looked at the picture of herself, Mimi, and Tasha that sat on her nightstand. She wiped them away, took a deep breath, and picked it up. "Mimi," she whispered as her fingers traced the faces in the picture. "God, please take care of my girl."

Honk! Honk!

The sound of Malek's car horn made her jump. She put the picture in the basket and took one last look at her room before turning out the light.

Tasha was waiting in the hallway, leaning against the wall. With her arms folded in front of her, she looked defiant.

Honk!

"I've got to go," Halleigh stated reluctantly.

Tasha nodded and said, "It's on, bitch! I should whup your ass right now! Hmm."

"Take care of yourself, Tash," Halleigh stated through her tears. She took her house key off her key ring and held it out for Tasha.

"Get that shit out my face before I wear your ass out," she replied, slapping the key out of Halleigh's hand.

Halleigh left the house in tears and in shock and walked back to the car.

"You a'ight?" Malek asked. He noticed that she had been crying, and he reached out for her hand.

She gripped it tightly. "Let's go," she whispered as she looked up at the apartment building.

Malek put the car in gear and pulled away from Halleigh's past. "Halleigh, what's up? What's wrong? What happened in there?"

Halleigh slumped in her seat and blew some air out of her lungs. "I don't know . . . she talking crazy. It's like I go from Manolo and one controlling situation to another. Like she don't want me to leave, talking about if I leave, then it's on. '*It's on, bitch!*'" Halleigh said in a mocking tone. "I mean, I can't believe her."

"Halleigh, it's done! You outta here and you ain't looking back."

Halleigh didn't respond immediately to Malek.

"You trust me to take care of you, right?"

Halleigh hesitated, and then she looked at Malek and said, "Malek, you know I trust you, you know that. But I wanna ask you something, and I need you to be straight-up and completely honest with me."

"Definitely," Malek responded.

"Malek, did you kill Mimi and Tasha's brother Maury?" Halleigh asked with a frown and a concerned look.

Malek cut his eyes at Halleigh, trying to figure out how she could have known that. He was also wondering just how he should answer her, so he kept quiet. His hope was that through his silence, Halleigh would get the answer she was looking for.

Halleigh asked again, "Malek, did you kill Mimi and Maury?"

Malek reached forward and turned up the volume to Jay-Z's *American Gangster* soundtrack. But he made sure not to answer Halleigh's question.

Chapter Three

"Manolo's money is my money, and you fucked up Manolo's money. So that means you fucked up my money!" Sweets bitch-slapped Tasha, sending her to the floor of the beauty salon.

Tasha had reached out to Sweets, asking him to meet her at the hair salon. Her hope was that if she were to meet him in a public place, he wouldn't spazz out on her. But with the loss of her brother and one of her best friends, she was really going through it, and she decided to return to the one thing that was familiar to her: selling pussy.

Sweets held his foot to Tasha's throat, completely cutting off her air. "Where the fuck was you?"

As Tasha was about to pass out, Sweets finally relented. He grabbed her by her hair and dragged her out of the hair salon and into his waiting Yukon Denali. "Get yo' ass in that truck!"

Tasha got in the truck, and Sweets got in the backseat with her and instructed his driver to take off. He reached in his waistband and pulled out his 9 mm and pressed the barrel of the gun against her forehead.

"Bitch, you better start talking, and you better make that shit good!"

Tasha was so nervous that she was about to wet her pants. At that moment, she was second-guessing her decision to want to reach out to Sweets and Manolo.

"Sweets, I know how it looks, but as soon as I could reach out and say what was up without getting killed, that's exactly what I did. Officer Troy is a dirty muthafucka and snatched up me, Mimi, and Halleigh, and threatened to lock our asses up and to kill us if we didn't get down with what he was gonna do.

"We didn't know exactly what he was plotting, but now I know what was up. Halleigh and her snake ass had been down with Malek from the North Side, and she put Malek up on how Manolo was moving. Malek worked it out with Officer Troy to rob Manolo, which was all part of Malek and Jamaica Joe's plan to take over the South Side. Malek promised Troy way more than he could turn down, so Troy went with it.

"Then I find out people is dropping like flies. Mimi got hit, and my brother got hit, but meanwhile shit is looking good for Halleigh. So I put two and two together, and I find out that Malek done murked my brother and Mimi, and that's when I knew what was up.

"I said fuck Officer Troy and his bullshit threats, 'cause I knew that I was next to get killed. So it was either I get killed by officer Troy, I get locked up by officer Troy, I get killed by Malek, or I risk my life and reach out to you and Manolo and tell y'all what's up and try to get back on this madame grind! You feel me?" Tasha said all in one breath. Trying to come across as convincing, she was rambling nonstop like a chickenhead. But that was because she was nervous and because she knew that her life was seconds from being snuffed out.

Still holding the gun to her head, Sweets squinted his eyes as he looked at her.

"Sweets, tonight I can get this ho shit back on and poppin'! I'll sell my pussy and I can get that chick Keesha who been trying to get down with Manolo from day one. Come on, just let me get this money for you, Sweets."

"Bitch, I should throw your ass out this moving car right now 'cause you playing me for a bitch-ass nigga."

"Sweets, I'll get Officer Troy on the phone right now. I'll put him on speaker, and you'll see for yourself that I ain't lying."

Tasha was lying through her teeth, but she was desperate and she just hoped like hell that Sweets didn't call her bluff because, if he did, she knew that he wouldn't hesitate to pop her ass.

Sweets, eyes still on Tasha, lowered his gun.

Tasha exhaled.

"So Malek is really trying to be Frank Lucas, *American Gangster* in this bitch?"

"Sweets, his ass is so lame! He running around like a gangsta, and meanwhile half the city done ran up in his girl that he's treating like wifey. And this nigga ain't never even screwed Halleigh yet? Bitch ass!"

Tasha's words made Sweets chuckle to himself.

"That nigga must be waiting for me to bend his ass over and lay some pipe to 'im," Sweets said in a sinister tone. His dick actually began to swell at the mere thought of being able to do a tender young enemy like Malek.

Tasha, like everybody else, was disgusted with Sweets and his homo-thug behavior. But she would much rather see Malek get raped and killed by Sweets than to see herself laying dead in the streets at the hands of Manolo or Sweets. In fact, she knew that Sweets would be the one to avenge the death of her brother and Mimi, who was like a sister to her. Like she had told Halleigh, *It's on!*

Chapter Four

Malek sat in the limo along with Jamaica's Joe's baby mother and their two young sons while on the way to the funeral services. Malek supported Joe's family during this devastating time. Sobs and lost hopes filled the air, and it broke Malek's heart to see Jamaica Joe's young sons, smiling and playing, not grasping that their father was gone forever.

Just the day before, Malek had found out Joe had a baby mother and kids. Joe always preached to Malek about keeping family and business completely separate. Obviously, Joe used to practice what he preached, because Malek had no idea that he had a family.

Although Malek didn't know about Joe's family, Joe made sure that his wife always knew who to reach out to and what to say in the event of his untimely death or imprisonment.

Malek made a mental note to remember and

utilize the game that Joe had given him during their relationship. A chill went through his body as he saw Joe's grieving woman sobbing while sitting across from him.

Kim, Jamaica Joe's woman, kept whispering while quietly crying into a handkerchief, "He's gone, he's gone."

Malek rested his hand on her shoulder and assured her that he would retaliate against the man that killed her man. She kept asking Malek what went on that night and he told her everything, leaving out the mysterious woman, not wanting to throw dirt on Joe's name. She had enough worries; Malek didn't want to reveal that Joe was cheating on her in the process.

"Everything is going to be all right," Malek said confidently. He looked through the window and noticed that they had reached the church. His heart dropped when he saw the pallbearers unloading Joe's casket from the hearse. The death of Jamaica Joe had the whole city in mourning. The city had just lost one of its elite, and all of the hood legends, crackheads, workers, and community were in attendance to pay their final respects to Flint's fallen boss.

Joe had taken a page out of Mob boss John Gotti's life. Like Gotti, Joe would always throw neighborhood barbecues, give turkeys on Thanksgiving, gifts on Christmas, not to mention fireworks on the Fourth of July for the whole neighborhood to enjoy. And although the citizens knew that he was a dangerous drug dealer, they all loved him.

Because of his constant benevolence, they always overlooked his misdeeds.

Malek and Joe's family stepped out the limo onto and the packed sidewalk, where people crowded the streets outside of New Jerusalem Church. They walked into the church to say their final good-byes.

Malek took a deep breath. He patted his waist to make sure his gun was in place before he entered the church. He saw firsthand what could happen when you put your guard down, and he vowed to himself to never get caught slipping again. *I'm never taking any more bullets again. That's my word. I'm going to body a nigga before they body me,* Malek thought as he felt the tenderness in his shoulder from the gunshot wound.

Malek knew that Joe's funeral was littered with undercover cops and federal agents who likely wanted to question him, but he didn't care at that point, because everything was about Joe. And with the way he was feeling, he knew that he would probably go to jail for murdering a cop with his bare hands if they were to be disrespectful and approach him at Joe's funeral.

The walk to Joe's casket seemed like it was three miles long to Malek. He looked down at Joe's body and was at a loss for thoughts and words. Seeing a man that was so powerful lying in a casket taught him a lesson—nobody was untouchable.

After the service, Malek sat with the family at Joe's estate just outside Flint, in the suburb of Grand Blanc. Malek never knew that Joe had a spot in Grand Blanc. He knew about Joe's spot in Flint, but never knew that he also rested in Grand Blanc. With Joe being dead, Malek figured that it didn't matter anymore who knew where Joe lived. See, Joe was a certified gangsta from the old school, and he knew that once a player in the game was either murdered or locked up, the player's family would be off-limits to his enemies at that point.

Only there to show moral support for Joe's family, Malek was quiet and to himself. He stared out of the living room window, thinking about how Joe took him under his wing. Joe showed him how to be a thinking man and to always plan his moves. That's why Malek was already thinking about getting to Sweets. Retaliation was a must for him.

All of Joe's henchmen and former workers were scattered around the room, grieving in sorrow. Malek felt someone gently rest a hand on his shoulder, and he turned to see Kim.

"Hey."

"Hey. How you holding up?" Malek asked as he faced her.

"I can't believe he's gone. He was just talking about leaving here for good. He promised me that once he got you situated and prepared you to take over the empire, he was gone."

Malek dropped his head, as a wave of guilt overcame him.

Kim gently lifted his head with her index finger and stared him in the eyes. "It's not your fault," she said. "Joe was his own man and made his own decisions." She grabbed Malek's hands. "Look around this room, Malek. You got an army that's willing to do whatever you say. You have power by default. You are in charge now. But with this game comes death, jail, and sorrow. Don't let this game swallow you. Get out! Get out now, before it's too late."

Kim's eyes teared up. She saw firsthand how the game altered Joe's mind, so that even though he had enough money to leave the game, he didn't. She witnessed how the allure of the game kept him in the streets, which ultimately led to his premature demise. She felt obligated to warn Malek of the flip side of the game; the cons of the drug game. Malek reminded her so much of Joe, and she saw the same glare in Malek's eyes that once was in Joe's.

Kim reached in her bosom and pulled out a small key and a small piece of paper that had a safety deposit box number on it. "Malek, I'm supposed to hand this key to you. But it rips at me to do it because it's like me signing your death certificate."

"Whatchu talking about? Ain't nobody bringing death to me!" Malek said defiantly.

Kim shook her head. She knew that Malek had that gangsta ego, which was one of the worst kind. "Malek, listen, just tell me you don't want this key because you're about to get out of the game and you won't need it."

Malek smirked. He looked down at the ground and then at Kim.

"Kim, I'm supposed to be in the NBA right now.

But I fucked that up and I didn't make it. And in the process, I let my agent down, I let my fans down, I let my coaches down. And you wouldn't believe how I let my moms down. But you know what? There isn't anybody that I let down more than myself! So for me to walk away from you right now and not take that key, a key that Joe wanted me to have, then you know what? I would be letting Joe down and proving how much of a fuck-up and a failure I am."

"Malek, I hear you. And you know, you're about to make tears come to my eyes. You were gonna be the number one pick in the NBA and now you're about to be the number one hustler in Flint. But what you're missing is that you could be number one in whatever you put your mind to. Start a business and you'll be bigger than Bill Gates. Go to law school and you'll be bigger than Johnnie Cochran. And that's because you got something special in you just like Joe had. Don't follow in Joe's footsteps and waste that special gift that God put in you."

Malek paused as if he were in deep thought, and he did take in every word that Kim had said. But he felt that she didn't really understand him and that she never would, nor would anyone else. He moved forward and embraced her, and he whispered in her ear and told her to be strong. As he hugged her, he simultaneously took hold of her hand and the key that was his.

"I'll be smarter," he said to her.

She nodded her head, knowing that she was handing him death.

About a week after Jamaica Joe's funeral, Malek walked into the First of America Bank, the place where Joe kept his safety deposit box. It had been two weeks since he'd been shot, and he was ninety percent healed from his wounds. Malek wondered what was in the safe deposit box and why Joe had told Kim to give the key to Malek if something ever happened to him. *It seemed like he knew he was going to die early*, Malek thought as he walked up to the male teller.

"Hello, how may I help you?" the man asked with a cheesy smile.

"I would like to go into my safety deposit box," Malek said as he slid the teller the card with the box number.

"Follow me," the man said as he made his way to the back of the bank. Malek followed the teller into the spacious vault.

The teller stuck his master key in the safety box and began to head out of the vault. "Ring the bell when you are ready to exit," he said before closing the vault behind him.

Malek slowly walked to the box and entered his key. He slowly turned it and pulled out the large steel box from the wall. He took the heavy box over to the table in the middle of the room.

Malek didn't know what to expect as he stared

at the box. He took a deep breath and opened it up. His eyes lit up as the neatly placed Benjamin Franklins lined up in stacks. He flipped through the money, all hundred-dollar bills. "Oh my God," he whispered.

A note with Malek's name on it was in an envelope under one of the money stacks. Malek picked it up and opened it.

Malek,

If you're reading this, that means I'm gone. Every hustler's reign eventually comes to an end. The lifestyle that we live doesn't come with any guarantees or pension plans. It's hard for a man to express his feelings to another man. It's just our nature. But I wanted to let you know that I love you like a younger brother. I see myself in you, and I want you to remember all the things that I taught you.

I don't want to tell you what to do or anything, but my greed probably is the reason why I'm not alive anymore. Get your money and get out of the game, Malek. If you stay too long, you will end up like me or in somebody's jail cell. Start you a family and enjoy the good things in life.

I left you one million dollars to secure your well-being. I am the one who turned you out to the streets; I feel it's only right to give you this. I put the poison in your hands and cursed you with a hustler's mentality. I never seen a hustler as smart or as disciplined as you. I created a monster. I can't tell you what to do with it, but please be smart. Re-

*member to keep business and personal completely
separated. Take care of yourself, Malek.*

                    One,
                    "Jamaica" Joe Holland

Malek took a deep breath and put the letter in
his pocket. He wasn't ready to leave the game
alone so soon. He had to admit that he didn't expect to be reading a note like that from Joe, but it
was what it was. Nobody knew what it was like to be
destined for the NBA and then to have that pulled
from under you. Nobody understood what it was
like to have things at your beck and call from the
age of twelve simply because you can play ball. It
was like a drug to Malek, a drug that only a hand-
ful of human beings ever experienced. Malek had
experienced it, and he got addicted to it.

He wanted to feel that high again. He didn't
want to fuck the beauty queen and not climax. He
wanted to fuck the beauty queen and nut all over
her ass. And he hadn't nutted yet. As far as he was
concerned, he wouldn't bust that nut until he had
totally dominated the drug game in the same way
he'd dominated the game of basketball.

Yeah, Malek knew that he had unfinished business, like murdering Sweets on Joe's behalf, and
also making more money than Joe had ever imagined. He was going to learn from Joe's mistakes
and become bigger and better than him. It was
Malek's time.

Chapter Five

Malek had never seen so much money in his entire life. One million dollars lay scattered across his bed. He was giddy on the inside. When Malek had seen all of the cash inside of the safe deposit box, he almost came on himself at the sight of so much dough. He had to make three trips back to the bank in order to retrieve all of the cash. He didn't want to draw attention to himself, so each time he came back to the safe deposit box, he only carried a medium-size duffle bag with him to put the cash inside. He had been making money hustling, but Jamaica Joe had been "getting it," and the evidence of Joe's success in the game was right in front of him.

Malek had more than enough money to cop from Fredro. He was about to hit the streets hard, and no one, not even Sweets, was going to stop his rise to the top.

He counted the money for hours, verifying repeatedly that all of it was there. It wasn't a task for him. The money felt good in his hands. He knew that he couldn't act on his impulse to splurge frivolously. He was about to turn the one million into an empire and make his mentor proud. And without a doubt, Malek knew that he had to get back at Sweets, but he didn't want to move on him just yet. He first wanted to get his paper stacked as high as he could stack it, and then he wanted to catch Sweets sleeping.

Halleigh was silent as she lay across the bed in just her panty and bra set. She couldn't believe the riches that were scattered around her, but she was glad that Malek trusted her around his money.

Malek loved Halleigh's body and was always turned on by her. He regretted it regularly that he had never sexed her like they had planned on doing on the night that she was raped.

Truth be told, he wasn't that pressed to hit it now. See, the way he figured things, getting pussy wasn't a problem for him. He had a string of chicks that he had ran up in, and he could add to that list at his will. But the reason he hadn't been that pressed to hit it was because, ever since Halleigh had been raped, he looked at her as being defiled. Sort of like a bird with a broken wing, or a Mercedes that had been wrecked. And then on top of that, Halleigh had been a whore who got paid to get fucked.

Malek never let Halleigh in on his thoughts about why he was more than willing to be patient.

He wanted to come across as if he was being patient for her sake, while he was really being patient because he was trying to come to grips with the fact that her pussy was no longer special. She could have been infected with some type of disease, and on top of that, he was trying to figure out how he could make her his top bitch after she had basically been the whole hood's bottom bitch.

Fuck it! he thought as he took off his LRG jeans and his shirt and lay next to Halleigh on the bed along with all of the money. Without warning, he began kissing on her.

Halleigh loved the way Malek kissed her, and she loved the way his tongue felt in her mouth. She began to kiss him more passionately.

Malek slid his left hand onto Halleigh's pussy and began to rub on it through her panties.

"Emmmmhhh," Halleigh sighed with pleasure.

Malek was actually surprised that she hadn't tried to push him away or move his hand from her crotch like she normally had done. She usually ran a line on him that she wasn't ready to go there with him. Malek never pressured her, yet he never could understand how she would push him away as if she was a virgin, even though she had been with more dudes than Heather Hunter.

"I want you," Malek seductively whispered into Halleigh's ear as he kissed on her earlobe.

Halleigh didn't respond, so Malek took that as his cue to continue. He slid her panties off and quickly undid her bra, leaving her completely naked. He thought about going down on her, but then he decided against it. He just wanted to get to it before she changed her mind.

Malek was definitely turned on, and that was evident by the way his dick was standing at attention. He quickly slid off of his boxers and his shirt and stood there looking at Halleigh with nothing on but his Jesus piece dangling from his neck. Malek had a habit of always fucking in his Air Force Ones or his Timbs, but he usually did that with chicks he didn't respect. So he didn't fuck her with his sneakers on.

Malek spread Halleigh's legs apart and slowly slid his dick into her pussy, which was soaking wet and throbbing at this point. Malek was kind of surprised that Halleigh's walls gripped his dick so tightly. He was expecting her to be as loose as a Ziploc garbage bag.

"Damn, baby, your pussy feel so good," he said as he began to pump his dick in and out of her.

Halleigh tried her hardest not to tense up and think about the brutal rape that she had endured. She wanted to relax, and she hoped that Malek would truly enjoy her more than any other chick that he had ever been with.

"You really like it?"

Malek nodded his head up and down and continued pumping. Halleigh felt so good, she knew that Malek was gonna make her cum. Without warning, tears began to stream down her face.

"What's wrong, baby?" Malek asked.

"Nothing," Halleigh replied as she wiped her

tears away. "I just can't believe how much I love you and how good you're making me feel right now. I never felt this close to anybody before."

"I'm not going nowhere, baby," Malek said. "You trust me?" he asked as he pumped his dick harder and harder.

"Yes! Yes! Baby, I trust you," Halleigh replied as she began to gyrate her hips and contract her walls on Malek.

Malek had never had a chick contract her muscles the way Halleigh was doing. "Wow, baby, you're gonna make me cum! Oh shit! Your pussy feels good!"

Hearing Malek say those words to her was enough to make Halleigh explode.

"Oh, baby," Halleigh screamed. "I'm cumming!" She wrapped her legs around Malek and urged him to do it harder.

Malek followed her orders and pumped her so hard that he thought he was going to break the bed. Within thirty seconds, he pulled out and came.

"Whoa!" Halleigh said. "Malek, I never came so hard before! I feel dizzy!" She began laughing.

Malek laughed and told her how good he felt. He then went to retrieve a towel so that he could wipe off Halleigh's stomach.

Halleigh and Malek lay on the bed holding each other. Neither of them said a word, but both of them were thinking the same thing. They were thinking just how good life could have been had their lives never taken such a crazy turn.

* * *

"What are you going to do?" Halleigh asked finally after hours and hours of counting money that they had just finished having sex on top of.

She was hoping that Malek would say that he was going to take the money and get out of the game, so that the two of them could live the way they had envisioned when they were still in high school. She knew that they had enough money to live the same way an NBA contract would have allowed them. They had just had great sex, which would definitely continue, so in her mind, she couldn't see why Malek would want to continue in the drug game.

Malek looked at Halleigh and smiled. He remembered a valuable lesson that Jamaica Joe had taught him while he was alive. "Keep your business and personal life completely separated," he whispered to himself. He had the potential to give her the world, just as he had always promised. She was finally his, and he was going to take every precaution to keep her comfortable and safe. At the same time, he also knew to trust absolutely no one unless he wanted to risk a downfall. He still had never figured out how Halleigh knew that he had killed Maury and Mimi, and he left that subject alone. But in his mind, he had to be smart and keep his mouth shut so that he could protect himself, his hustle, and Halleigh.

Malek knew that he had to move Halleigh out of the hood. She needed to be untouchable, separated from his life in the streets. "I want you to go out and find us a house in a nice neighborhood. We can't stay up in here for too much longer. Niggas know where I rest at, and with this much money, I'm not taking no chances at becoming somebody's target."

"I can really pick any house I want?" Halleigh asked in excitement.

"Anything you want. You got a quarter million to play with," Malek stated.

"Two hundred fifty thousand dollars!" Halleigh exclaimed as she jumped up from the bed.

Malek laughed at her and pulled her close, kissing her on the lips. "Yeah, but make sure you get everything we need with that. Furniture and all," he answered.

"Can I start today? Can you take me house shopping?" she asked.

"Nah, I got some things I need to take care of. You playing with some paper, ma. Go buy yourself a whip."

"Seriously?" she asked.

"Yeah, for real. You gon' need your own car, so go buy one. Leave the money here in the safe, though. I'll take you to the car lot so you can pick out a car. When you find a house you like, just call me and I'll bring the cash," he said. Malek knew that there was more to buying a house than just bringing the cash, but what he was trying to do was let Halleigh know that she didn't have to want for anything or worry about a thing, because he had it like that.

Malek drove Halleigh to every car lot in the city

in search of a car she liked, and in three hours flat, she purchased a 2008 Nissan Maxima. Malek tried to talk her into buying a Benz, but she wanted to save the majority of the money for their house. She was satisfied with the $25,000 car because it left her with more funds to splurge on her dwelling.

Malek leaned into her window, and the smile on her face told him that she was worth the money he had put aside to take care of her.

"I'll call you when I find the house," she stated.

"A'ight. Be careful," he replied before she pulled out of the car lot full speed.

The first thing that Malek did was find himself a lawyer. He needed to wash his dirty money so that his large purchases wouldn't draw any unwanted attention from the alphabet boys; the last thing he wanted was the IRS and the feds on his back. He reached out to Jamaica Joe's lawyer, the same lawyer who had gotten him off on the bodega robbery, told him his situation, and asked him if he knew of any attorneys that he could refer him to. He was referred to Jacob Hill, one of the best criminal defense and financial advisement lawyers in the city.

Malek made his way across town to see attorney Jacob Hill and walked into a two-story building in his Pelle Pelle jeans and red-and-white team jacket with the matching fitted cap. His thuggish appearance was out of place in the corporate office, and the secretary eyed him suspiciously as he stepped to greet her.

"I'm here to see Jacob Hill," he stated smugly as he adjusted the cap on his head.

"Did you make an appointment?" she asked snootily.

"Nah, but he want to take this meeting with me. I'm about to bring him a lot of money," he replied as he sat down and leaned back in his chair. Malek told her which attorney had referred him to Jacob Hill.

The receptionist picked up the phone, all the while looking at Malek with contempt. "Mr. Hill, a young man is here to see you. He says it's important that you meet with him." The woman was quiet for a moment as she listened to her boss respond. She hung up the phone a moment later and said, "He'll be right out for you."

Malek nodded his head and waited until the attorney came out.

Jacob Hill walked from the back of the office and extended his hand toward Malek.

Malek stood and shook his hand. "Hello, Mr. Hill, I'm—"

"Malek Johnson," the attorney stated, finishing Malek's sentence. "I remember you from your basketball days."

From the look on his face, it was clear that he also remembered all the headlines about Malek's fall from grace.

"Yeah, that was a long time ago. I'm here for another matter," Malek stated.

"Well, come on back to my conference room," Mr. Hill invited.

Malek followed him through the office and into a room that contained a large red oak table.

"What can I do for you?"

Malek took a seat and replied, "I'm going to be frank with you. I need an attorney that likes to make money. Do you like money, Mr. Hill?"

The attorney adjusted his necktie nervously. "Well, who doesn't?" he answered.

"I have some cash, a large amount of cash, that I need to show a source for," Malek stated. "And I need a good lawyer to make sure I don't encounter certain aspects of the law."

"Well, that type of service doesn't come cheap," the attorney stated, trying to see what type of wealth Malek was working with.

"Will a quarter mill take care of it?"

The attorney's eyes widened at the amount of money.

"I'm trying to put you on payroll. I need to rely on you to make sure everything stays legit and accounted for," Malek said.

"You've got a deal," the attorney replied.

The two men discussed Malek's options, and Malek also expressed his expectations to his lawyer. Jacob Hill assured Malek that by the end of the week, he would be the owner of several profitable small businesses around the state of Michigan.

Malek knew that the only reason things had flowed so smoothly for him was because of the relationship that Jamaica Joe had with his attorney. Jamaica Joe's attorney had hipped Jacob Hill to how profitable it would be to have a major drug dealer as a client.

The attorney guaranteed that he would provide the financial statements and legal documents proving that Malek had been a major shareholder in a thriving business for the past three years.

By having a solid, successful company, Malek was free to purchase whatever he wanted, whenever he wanted, without raising anyone's suspicions. Well, it wasn't actually free; it cost Malek a quarter of a million just to get in the door with Jacob Hill, as well as an ongoing 10 percent of the laundered money going to Jacob Hill. The money he spent and would continue to spend to make it all happen was well worth it. It ensured his freedom and gave him an ally that was skilled in the art of interpreting the law.

That same night, Malek put in the call to Fredro to pick up forty kilos of cocaine. He purchased the bricks at ten thousand apiece. After the house, the lawyer fees, and copping the coke, he would only have one hundred fifty thousand dollars left, but Malek was more than confident that he was about to come into his own.

The North Side had been in an uproar ever since Jamaica Joe's death. It had only been a couple days, but Malek knew that he had to take control over his hood. Niggas were getting money on what were once Joe's blocks, and Malek was about to claim what was rightfully his. He knew who he needed to see.

Mitch was a hustler on the North Side of Flint, a young nigga who was doing his thing, but could never do too much when Joe was alive. Mitch had taken advantage of the open market and put his young boys to work on the North Side. Malek respected his hustle, and wanted Mitch on his team. He knew that recruiting Mitch was the first move in this big game of chess he was about to play. He was about to take over the streets.

He drove through the hood in his Lincoln Navigator and came up on some of Mitch's workers who were posted up in front of Mitch's dope house. Malek sat his burner in his lap, just in case one of the young boys wanted to jump stupid. Then he rolled down his window and tapped on his horn to get the crowd's attention.

"Yo, my man. Come here," Malek shouted to one of the workers.

The young boy's eyes shifted nervously as he debated whether or not to approach Malek. His friends looked skeptically in Malek's direction.

"Look, li'l niggas, I got five stacks for whoever can deliver a message to Mitch for me," Malek called out.

The boys still hesitated, but one walked out of the pack. His jeans were low on his behind, and one hand was on his belt buckle. Half of his hair was braided, while the other half was all over his head.

"Shit, I'll make this money," he commented as he trotted over to Malek's car. "Yo, you for real, fam?" the boy asked as he stood at Malek's window.

Malek tossed a rolled-up wad of money out of the window and said, "Tell Mitch that Malek needs to holla at him about something. Let him know it's all love, though. Tell him to get at me sooner rather than later too." Malek didn't wait for the boy to respond. He put his car in drive and cruised down the block.

When Malek entered the house at around three in the morning, Halleigh was sleeping soundly on her side of the bed. The feeling he experienced when he saw her assured him that he still loved her. She was like a breath of fresh air. He stripped down to his boxers, placed his pistol on the night-stand, and slid underneath the covers next to her. He wrapped her in his arms, arousing her slightly.

"Umm, I found a house today," she whispered groggily.

"Oh yeah? How much is it?" he asked.

"One fifty," she responded without opening her eyes. "Can you come see it tomorrow?"

"Yeah, we'll go first thing in the morning. Get some sleep."

Halleigh didn't respond, and her rhythmic breathing indicated that she had fallen back to sleep.

The next morning, Malek fulfilled his promise and escorted her to the house that she had chosen. To Malek's surprise, Halleigh had found a four-bedroom, two and a half bath in the prestigious suburb of Grand Blanc.

"Why is it so cheap?" he asked the realtor that was showing them around. He knew that houses started at $200,000 in that neighborhood.

"It's being foreclosed on. It was an older retired couple that lived here on a fixed income. They ran into some medical bills and decided to refinance their home, and after doing so, they couldn't keep up with the new payments. But, hey, this is really an excellent buy. Unfortunately someone else's pain will now be your gain. You may have to redecorate on the inside. Like I'd just stated, an older retired couple lived here, so the décor is a bit outdated, and the pool in the back needs some work, but everything else in the house is in mint condition."

Malek admired the spacious layout of the house. He looked down at Halleigh. "You want it?" he asked her.

She nodded while smiling and replied, "I do. I know it looks old and funky on the inside, but I can do all of the remodeling and decorating myself. I can make it ours."

"We'll take it," Malek stated. "I'll be paying cash. How soon can we get the keys?"

The realtor looked surprised and also excited about the prospect of a quick sale. "I can have the paperwork completed for you by the end of today, and if you want, you can take possession of it first thing tomorrow."

"Yeah, okay. Let's do that," Malek stated as he held onto Halleigh's hand.

Halleigh clapped happily and jumped up and down in excitement. "I can't believe it. Now I have to go to Home Depot to pick out new carpeting."

Malek laughed at her rambling and guided her out of the house.

They spent the remainder of the day picking out furniture and appliances, and hiring contractors to update the house. By the end of the day, the paperwork was signed, and they were packing up Malek's apartment.

The next day, Malek hired movers to relocate their possessions. Halleigh was directing the traffic that was coming in and out of the small apartment, while Malek oversaw the activities. He noticed an old-school black Monte Carlo with tinted windows sitting up the block. Malek had a feeling that there was someone in the car watching him.

After fifteen minutes of eyeing the car, paranoia kicked in. He didn't want to alarm Halleigh, so he didn't tell her what was going on. He knew that if somebody was watching his crib, then they were targeting him.

He walked into the house slowly as he continued to stare up the street at the parked car.

"Hal!" he yelled.

Halleigh walked toward him. "What up?" she asked.

"I'm about to go to the store. You want something?"

"Nah, I'm good, babe," she responded as she

kissed him quickly and then went about her business.

Malek strolled outside, his five-carat Jesus piece glistening against his fitted white T-shirt as he jogged over to his Navigator. He reached underneath his seat and retrieved his burner. His temperature was through the roof. He couldn't believe a nigga had the nerve to plot on him. "I know they ain't trying to bring heat to my home," he said to himself as he took his gun off safety.

He pulled out of the driveway and drove in the direction of the idle car. He sped up until he was directly beside the Monte Carlo and then jumped out, leaving his car running. He snatched open the passenger side door and pressed the pistol to the passenger's head.

"Ohh shit! fam, hold up! Fall back, my nigga, damn!" he heard the driver state. "Malek, chill out!"

Malek aimed his pistol toward the driver and was surprised to see Mitch sitting there with a blunt in his hand.

"Fuck you watching me for?" Malek demanded.

"Fam, you came through the hood looking for me. I was just coming to check you out to see what was up. Damn!"

The passenger in the car was holding his face and groaning in pain.

"Nigga, you posted up the block from my crib like you lurking. My woman rests her head up in there. What the fuck were you sitting so long for?" Malek yelled.

Mitch held up the burning blunt that was still in his hand and stated, "We was getting blowed. Damn."

Malek finally tucked his gun back in his pants and shook his head. "My fault, fam."

"You got my man over here all shook," Mitch said. "What's good? You came through the hood and paid my li'l man five stacks. You got them thinking you boss, fam." Mitch's tone was light and joking, but Malek could sense the seriousness in his voice.

"Come spin the block with me for a minute," Malek stated.

"I'll be right back," Mitch told the guy in his car, who frowned at Malek.

"My fault," Malek stated, finally acknowledging the passenger that he had roughed up. The guy didn't respond, but Malek didn't care. *He shouldn't have been posted in front of my crib,* he thought without remorse as a smirk crossed his face.

Mitch caught his expression and burst into laughter. "You wrong for fucking that nigga up like that," Mitch commented as he continued to laugh.

They hopped into Malek's car, and he pulled away.

"I know you know you hustling my blocks," Malek said, no malice in his voice, but his tone serious.

"I'm hustling. And I know you used to roll with Joe, but I don't know too much about them blocks being yours," Mitch responded.

"Look, I ain't against you getting money. What I'm against is you taking money out of my pocket and you pushing that bullshit-ass product on Joe's blocks—on my blocks. Now, I'm not trying to beef out with you. If we go to war, don't nobody make no dough, feel me?"

"Yeah, I hear that, fam," Mitch agreed.

"So why don't we just do this together?" Malek stated.

Mitch was reluctant. "No disrespect, but why would I split what I'm making?"

"Because I've got Joe's connect."

"Word?" Mitch said in shock.

"Look, I'm going to put it to you like this: You can get down or lay down. This is a movement what I'm about to do, and I want you on my team. If you not an ally, I'm going to consider you an enemy. I'm tryin'a give you a key to the world right now, fam."

"You actually got Joe's connect?" Mitch asked in disbelief. He knew that Joe had the best coke in the city for years and that no one could seem to match his product. On occasions, he'd even lied to some of his buyers, saying that he had got the raw from Joe, just to get the sell.

Malek smirked and replied, "Your tune sound like it done changed, fam. You in or you out? I need a right hand."

"I'm in, fam, I'm definitely in. Let's get this money," Mitch replied.

Malek nodded his head as he pulled back onto his street. He dropped Mitch off at his car and noticed that the passenger was still ice-grilling him. He got a bad aura from Mitch's man.

"I'ma get at you in a couple days," Malek said as he slapped hands with Mitch. "But first thing you need to do is get rid of that muthafucka. He got larceny in his heart. Nigga can't crank my product or be a part of nothing I'm doing."

Mitch nodded his head in agreement just before getting into his car.

Chapter Six

Over the next six months, Malek completely took over the city. He hadn't seen or heard from Sweets during his takeover. He got word from the streets that Sweets and his crew left town, and he was just waiting to hear from or see Sweets so he could send him to meet Joe.

But what Malek didn't know was that Sweets had hired an excellent attorney for Manolo. The attorney was able to subpoena the police department's video surveillance tapes of the precinct where Officer Troy worked. On those tapes they were able to go back to the date that Manolo's club had been raided, and they saw Tasha going into Officer Troy's office.

With the threat of Tasha being able to testify and further expose corruption within the Flint Police Department, the department was willing and able to spring Manolo from jail on technicalities—the major "technicality" being that it was an election year and Flint's incumbent mayor didn't need any new police scandals landing on the front page of the newspapers if he wanted to retain the slim chance he had of being re-elected.

So, with Manolo being sprung from the joint, he and Sweets were planning to take out Malek. They were just laying in the cut, waiting to catch him out there, high off of his own rising status in the game.

At a young age, Malek had accomplished what many hustlers could never reach: he had a supreme coke connect, an army of loyal henchmen, and intelligence. These were all ingredients to becoming a kingpin. Malek learned from Joe's mistakes and molded himself into a force to be reckoned with.

One of those mistakes that Malek had seen Jamaica Joe make was his disloyalty to Tariq. Although Malek had benefited from the favor and found himself in with Jamaica Joe, he was smart enough to realize that Tariq, by right, should have been in his position. But Jamaica Joe sort of passed Tariq over, and it brought problems to Joe that he wouldn't have had to deal with had he properly promoted the people who had been with him the longest.

Malek and Mitch were similar in more than one way, and they clicked instantly. Malek put Mitch in charge of the streets, while he managed the distribution and business side. Again, Malek knew that he had to keep Mitch's belly full, otherwise it would be Mitch who would soon be coming for

Malek's crown the same way Tariq had been gunning for Joe's.

Malek had managed to do what no other hustler in Flint had ever achieved, taking over the North and South Sides. He offered the best dope and the cheapest price, and like any successful businessman, created a brand, labeling his coke "Joe Blow." Everyone craved for it. He was getting it so cheap, he didn't have to mark it up too high, and eventually the empire spread into Detroit, Lansing, and other cities in Michigan.

Malek had quickly turned the $500,000 into $4 million in a small amount of time, his relationship with Halleigh was strong, and he had the streets on lock. Malek had recently purchased courtside season tickets to the Detroit Pistons, where he and Halleigh loved to spend their nights as a couple.

During the days, Halleigh was your typical kept woman. She wanted for nothing, drove high-end cars, and did a lot of shopping for clothes by designers with names that are hard to pronounce. But, in addition to being a diva, she was also very domesticated. She made sure she stayed on top of the numerous contractors that she'd hired to do renovations to their new home, and she also found the time to cook on a daily basis.

Malek felt on top of the world at that point. He even managed to recruit some of Sweets' old workers and place them under his organization. Everyone wanted to get a piece of the American dream, and with Malek's prices and high-quality product, they were more than able to.

Malek and Mitch were cruising down Clio Road in Malek's drop-top BMW, bobbing their heads in unison to 50 Cent's "I Get Money," which was blasting out of the subwoofers.

"Yo, I never seen this much money in my life, fam. We getting major paper, son!" Mitch clapped his hands together to emphasize his point.

"No doubt. We're going to continue to get it too. We have to just stick to the rules and keep a low profile. How is everything in the hood?" Malek asked as he pulled up into Popeye's Chicken.

"Everything is one hundred," Mitch answered. "Money is right, and everybody paying on time. Everyone except Big Petey in Selby hood. He like a week late on that last brick I hit him with."

"Word?" Then Malek said into the intercom, "Let me get a two-piece meal."

"Yep, the nigga talkin' greasy too, like he don't gotta pay on time because he was Joe's man." Mitch nodded his head up and down.

Malek had recruited Big Petey months before, because he knew that he was a good customer to Joe when he was alive. *He thinks because Joe ain't around anymore that shit is sweet. I see I'm going to have to make an example out of him quick,* Malek thought as he retrieved his food and pulled off on his way to pick up his money—from Petey.

* * *

"There go his hangout spot right there," Mitch said as he pointed down the street to Rube's Bar. Malek pulled his new BMW on the curb and got out. He and Mitch strolled down the block where the small bar was located. Malek and Mitch entered the dark bar, and just like Mitch said, Big Petey was in there. There were only three people in the whole bar: Petey, an old junkie in the back, and the owner, who stood behind the bar.

"What's going on, Rube?" Malek said as he sat at the bar, wiping off the counter.

"Malek! My man! What's going on, young-blood?" the overweight Rube said. Rube had owned his establishment for years and was known and respected in the community.

Malek remembered when Rube sponsored his youth team's jerseys when he was in middle school.

"What's up, Big Petey?" Malek asked as he watched Petey down a shot of Hennessy.

Petey didn't respond. He knew that Malek came to his spot to ask him about the money. He also noticed how Mitch was ice-grilling him. Big Petey instantly felt disrespected. Without even acknowledging Malek, he signaled for Rube to pour him another shot.

Rube, sensing the hostility, looked at Malek and then went over to pour Petey his shot.

Malek disregarded the blatant disrespect from Petey and continued to attempt to converse with him. "My man Mitch says that you owe me a li'l something."

"You got some nerve, coming to my block with some tough-guy shit. I been hustling since you been pissing in yo' diaper. Like I told that stupid muthafucka, I'ma hit you off when I get it. Damn!" Big Petey said as he downed the shot.

"Well, when do you think you going to have it?" Malek asked cool, calm, and collected.

Mitch moved his hand to his waist, where his pistol rested, and Malek quickly shook his head, signaling Mitch to fall back.

"I'll get it when I get it!" Big Petey yelled in a drunken slur.

Malek slowly got up, reached into his pocket, and pulled out a wad of money. He gently placed a hundred-dollar bill on the counter, and then, without any emotion on his face, looked at Petey. He said, "I am going to pick up my money in one week. One week exactly. The drinks are on me." Then he signaled Mitch to follow him out.

Malek winked at Rube and began to walk out, but before he reached the door, Big Petey said something under his breath—"Ol' bitch-ass nigga"—just loud enough for Malek to hear him.

Malek stopped dead in his tracks and, without even turning around, said, "Yo, Big Petey, you don't have to worry about that little bread you owe me." Malek walked toward the door, not to exit, but to lock the place up. He didn't want anybody to walk in while he was taking care of business.

Petey was so busy drinking his glass of Hennessy, he didn't notice Malek come back into the bar. Before Petey could react, Malek struck him over the head with a beer bottle. Petey awkwardly fell onto the floor, and without hesitation, Malek pulled out his gun and squeezed a round into Petey's face.

That was surely not the first time that Malek had to lay a person down for coming short on his money. He wasn't for games, and it was a new era. He was sending a clear message. It was a new sheriff in town. A sheriff with the balls to kill, and just like Malek had made it a point to up his street credibility by telling key street niggas that he had murked Mimi and Maury, he was sure to let the hood know that he had also dropped Petey. But Malek knew he had to be careful because with too much bravado came snitches, murder investigations, and jail time.

Chapter Seven

At the beginning of Game One of the NBA Eastern Conference finals between the Cleveland Cavaliers and the Detroit Pistons, it wasn't LeBron James or Rasheed Wallace who received the loudest applause from the sold-out Detroit Pistons crowd, but Malek Johnson.

Malek's face flashed on the big screen located inside the arena, and then the words *Michigan's Finest Is in the House* flashed underneath Malek's name, which was followed by highlights of dunks from Malek's sensational high-school career.

Malek loved every minute of the attention as he sat courtside with Halleigh. He had more than ten thousand dollars in cash in his pocket and was decked in jewelry worth upwards of one hundred thousand dollars. He and Halleigh were dressed in outfits that cost about two grand each, and they looked like movie stars who had the money to make sure their skin, teeth, and hair were cared for by highly paid professionals on a daily basis.

Malek nodded and raised his hand to the crowd and mouthed the words *Thank you*. An indescribable adrenaline rush consumed his body, and it felt so good. It reminded him of the high of being a superstar, a high that he hadn't felt in years.

As the players warmed up in preparation for the game, a player for the Pistons walked up to Malek and gave him a pound and a quick ghetto embrace. He shouted into Malek's hear, "You supposed to be out here. This is your house. Can't nobody on this court stop you."

Malek wasn't expecting such kind words of praise, and he definitely appreciated it.

"That's what's up!" Malek replied.

The crowd was still in a frenzy, screaming in anticipation of the game that was about to begin.

All throughout the game, Malek was constantly being tapped on his shoulder and handed a pen and a piece of paper and asked for his autograph.

"They always gonna love you, baby," Halleigh said to Malek as she kissed him on his cheek and snuggled close to him.

At halftime, an ESPN reporter and a cameraman came up to Malek and asked him if they could have a moment with him on camera.

"No doubt," Malek replied. By this time, Malek was buzzing from all of the Heineken he'd drunk.

"Malek, obviously you've had some bad breaks in terms of your career. Can you give the fans a little insight into the outlook on your future?" the reporter asked.

"Well, yeah, I mean I've had some unfortunate things happen to me, and I've come to grips with the fact that my career as an athlete is basically over," Malek said rather bluntly. "But don't get it twisted, and please understand that if I laced up some sneakers right now, I could go out and score fifty points against any team in this league."

"Wow! I see you still have the confidence that got you to be the most coveted player since LeBron James. But, Malek, how do you internalize that, and how does that make you feel?"

"I'm human, so obviously there's huge disappointment. So that's how it makes me feel. I feel disappointed. But how I internalize it is, I realize that I'll always be number one at whatever I do and whatever I set my mind to."

"Well, give the people a little update as to just what you have been doing with yourself since you put down the ball."

Malek reached into his pocket and pulled out the huge wad of money he was carrying. He laughed and then he replied, "I been getting this paper! Word! That's what I been doing. And you see these courtside seats that me and my baby got; these were a gift. I purchased these for the season. A hundred and twenty thousand for the year is what these seats ran me. And from this vantage point, the vantage point of a fan, I realize that I can actually aspire to own a team of my own.

"That's what I want the public to know. Know that

I won't be a tragic statistic. Nah, Malek Johnson is gonna be like Jay-Z. He went from hustling to owning a piece of the New Jersey Nets, and if he can do it, then so can I."

The reporter smiled and said, "Well, there you have it, folks, straight from the mouth of Malek Johnson, or shall I say soon-to-be NBA owner Malek Johnson."

Malek sat back down in his chair next to Halleigh and waited for the players to finish warming up so that the game could start. As Malek sat and thought, he realized that he actually could become an owner if he set his mind to it. He settled in his mind right then and there that he would indeed one day become an owner of an NBA team.

About a minute or so into the third quarter, Halleigh let out a sigh. "What the hell is that bitch doing here?" Halleigh asked as she saw Keesha walking toward her and Malek.

Keesha was sitting on the lower level of seats, about ten rows away from Malek and Halleigh. She began ice-grilling Halleigh as soon as she was able to get her attention. But Halleigh kept listening to Malek and paid Keesha no mind.

As soon as there was a real raucous part of the game, Keesha took advantage of the commotion and rushed past security. She ran up on Halleigh, yanked her to the ground, and began wailing on her.

Halleigh tried her best to fight back and fight off Keesha, but she wasn't strong enough. Keesha's first blow had caught her real good and made her woozy.

"The fuck is you doing?" Malek shouted as he kicked Keesha and then pulled her off Halleigh.

It took the spectators some time to realize what was going on, but as soon as they did, the crowd went into an uproar. The players were quickly rushed off the court, and security rushed to the fight in an attempt to break it up.

"You snitch-ass bitch!" Keesha screamed at Halleigh.

Some dude in a ski mask asked in a mocking tone, "Yo, Malek, can I have your autograph?" as he reached in his waistband and pulled out a gun and started firing in Malek's direction.

Malek didn't have his gat on him, so he couldn't return fire on the dude. He ducked and dove and grabbed Halleigh, and the two of them went crashing to the ground. With the sound of the gunshots, the entire arena went into a panic and headed for the exits.

"Baby, we gotta get the fuck outta here!" Malek shouted to Halleigh. "Come on! Stay low! Let's go!" He grabbed hold of Halleigh's hand, and the two of them rushed out of the arena amidst the chaos. All Malek could think of was getting to a safe spot so he could call his boys and tell them to strap up and get ready for war.

He knew that it was Sweets who had just sent a hitman to take him out in a very public place. Malek knew that he had to react and react quickly, especially since the whole world would now be talking about how Malek Johnson almost got killed at an NBA game.

Chapter Eight

"You did good, baby girl! Real good!" Manolo said to Keesha as she slurped, sucked, and stroked his dick.

Keesha shifted her eyes and looked up at Manolo, to see if he was enjoying her skills. "You like the way I suck your dick, daddy?"

"Yeah, daddy likes it, baby. Superhead ain't got shit on you! You'll do anything for daddy, right?"

Keesha nodded her head up and down to indicate that, now that she was officially a Manolo Mami, she would in fact do anything for Manolo. She was even willing to kill if she had to.

Manolo stood up from the chair and had Keesha get up off her knees so that he could fuck her doggy-style. Manolo loved Keesha's pussy. He couldn't figure out why he'd waited so long to put her down with his stable of bitches. But then he remembered that Keesha was the loud, screaming type that hollered and moaned, and carried on awhile.

See now, this screaming and hollering shit is gonna be bad for business, Tasha thought. She could hear Keesha hollering clear from the other side of the new townhouse that Manolo had rented for his stable of women.

Keesha was exactly the type of chick that Manolo needed around. Not only would she make him money by selling her pussy, but by kicking Halleigh's ass at that Detroit Pistons game, she had shown how much heart she had. And just as Sweets had used a woman to kill Jamaica Joe, Manolo and Sweets both knew that thirsty-ass Keesha would be their triggerwoman that would take out Malek.

As Manolo screwed Keesha, he kept pressing rewind on the DVR remote control so that he could keep replaying the news clip of Keesha pummeling Halleigh. "You beat that snake bitch's ass!" he said, laughing at the sight.

He pumped harder into Keesha, and she screamed louder than a virgin.

"You gonna kill that nigga for daddy, right?"

Keesha turned her head and looked at Manolo and screamed, "Yes!"

"That's what daddy's talking about!"

Manolo and Sweets both knew that things would be real hot for the next few weeks, so their plan was to just chill for a minute, and then they would make their move on Malek.

Keesha had been fucking a dude Mitch on a regular basis, and it just so happened to be the same Mitch that was now Malek's right-hand man. Keesha knew that Mitch was all about that almighty dollar and she would be able to flip him and get him to help her set up Malek. In her mind, it was just a matter of time before she would pull off the hit on Malek. She was certain that Manolo would elevate her over Tasha to be his top bitch. Finally, Keesha's ship was ready to come in.

Chapter Nine

Halleigh lay outside next to her pool, her Chloe glasses covering her eyes, and her two-piece Dolce swimsuit complementing her gold stilettos. Despite the recent drama, she was living how she always imagined she would.

Malek was wonderful and treated her with respect. The only thing that she didn't like was the fact that they didn't have sex all day, every day. Her body was aching in the worst way. She wanted Malek badly, but she was afraid that he'd look at her differently because she had been with so many men. His attitude didn't confirm her suspicions, but her suspicions were right on cue.

Yet still, Malek was damn near perfect. He was attentive and he spoiled her rotten. He was getting so much money that she was having a hard time spending it. He gave her a weekly allowance of $10,000 and she blew it on clothes, shoes, and jewelry. She had even saved up for two months and bought herself another car, a cherry red BMW convertible, which made her the envy of the town. She remodeled their entire house from top to bottom, and now she felt like she didn't have anything else to do. She was bored.

With Malek being in the streets, she was alone a lot. He kept late hours, which left her with a lot of time on her hands. She had been forced to end her friendship with Tasha and was lonely without her former partner in crime. Malek had literally secluded her from anyone and everyone that she knew, but she understood why. He had stepped into Jamaica Joe's shoes and was "that nigga" in the streets. Every bitch wished they could get their hands on him, and every nigga was trying to be down.

Being his woman made her a certified street diva, and she was playing her position well. She had gone from a Manolo Mami that any man could purchase, to a woman that no one could have. She was a hood legend. She was respected and talked about, but rarely seen. She was respected because Malek had upgraded her, and she was grateful for her new lifestyle.

The only time she ever went to the hood was to get her hair done. It was her one chance to catch up on everything that was happening on the North Side. When she first started going to the salons, she experienced "shade" from the North Side girls. By being a Manolo Mami, she was automatically looked at as competition by all of the South Side chicks like Keesha, who were thirsty to get down with Manolo. But once they found out about her and Malek, they warmed up to her.

She had so many associates, she couldn't even count, but she wasn't naïve. She knew that they were not her true friends. If anything, they just wanted to get close to her so that they could get the inside scoop on Malek and one day take her place. Halleigh would never set up her own fall from grace, so she kept all those thirsty bitches on a leash, staying close enough to know what they were thinking, but not close enough for them to know her thoughts. "Keep your friends close and your enemies closer," was her motto when it came to the gold-digging chicks she met on her way to the top.

Halleigh grabbed her silk robe and put it around her body before walking into her house. It was almost time for her hair appointment, so she headed inside to get dressed. She wore a yellow halter sundress with a yellow satin bow that tied around her waist. Yellow Aldo sandals with the wood-colored heel adorned her French mani-cured feet. Her hair was thick and nappy. She was definitely in need of a touch-up. She pulled her hair up in a loose ponytail, left her glasses on her face, and stepped out of her house.

Driving into the city, she bumped Keyshia Cole out of her custom speakers. She bobbed her head to the soul-searching lyrics. It was the middle of

the summer, so as soon as she entered the city lim-
its, she saw everybody out riding around in their
cars and chilling on the block. Halleigh loved the
attention that she got as she sped down Clio Road.
She parked in the parking lot to her favorite salon
and hopped out, engaging her car alarm as she
walked toward the building.

Halleigh was definitely living ghetto fabulous.
But everything in life came at a price. And in
Halleigh's case, there was a price to being the first
lady to the city's biggest hustler. For Halleigh, the
price that she had to pay was dealing with enemies, and especially the jealousy and envy of those
who wanted to have what she and Malek had.

So as Halleigh made her way into the salon, she
realized that for the first time in her life she was literally a bit paranoid. She thought, *What if Keesha
pops up again? Is Keesha now cool with Tasha, and if
so, is Tasha gonna come at me for what she looked at as
a lack of loyalty? Is Manolo still locked up, or is he out
on the streets? Would someone try to kill me for just being
Malek's girl?*

Yeah, Halleigh had stress to deal with, but she
tried her best to pamper herself at home and away
from home.

"Man, that young nigga ain't playin'. Scratch
saw the whole thang, ya dig. I mean, he just blew
that joker's brains out without even thinking about
it. Now pass me the pipe, nigga. You always hog-
gin' the rock," Scratch said as he conversed with

three of his crackhead friends who had huddled in the alley to split the twenty-dollar rock they had all put in on.

Scratch grabbed the crack-filled pipe from his associate and took a deep pull, letting the crack smoke rush down his throat and into his lungs. He noticed a person walking past the alley and jumped at the opportunity to hustle up on some more money.

Halleigh noticed a man coming from the alley.

When Scratch saw her approaching, he jumped up desperately. "Aww, pretty lady, pretty lady, can you give ol' Scratch some spare change?" he asked as he scratched the back of his small, dirty Afro.

"Scratch!" Halleigh yelled in excitement. Halleigh hadn't seen him in over a year and, oddly enough, was glad to see her old smoking buddy.

It was Scratch who had tried to push her away from heroin when she was looking for an emotional escape from her prostitution days with Manolo as her pimp. Scratch was a drug addict himself, so his trying to convince Halleigh to stay off heroin was like a cop trying to arrest himself. It wasn't gonna happen.

Halleigh and Scratch soon became get-high buddies. When Halleigh was getting high on an everyday basis in the alley with Scratch, she was at one of the lowest points in her life, on a runaway train, with death as her destination. Thankfully for her, Tasha was there for her and helped her to break her addiction.

"Li'l Rina?" Scratch said, calling her by the nickname he gave her because she reminded him so much of his other former smoking partner, Halleigh's mother, Rina. "That sho' is you. You look good, girl. Scratch heard you were messing with that young boy Malek. I heard he got you up in a big ol' pretty house in the suburbs somewhere. Ten bedrooms, twenty-eight bathrooms. Hell, even a golden shithole for the dog. You large, Li'l Rina! I'm proud of you."

Halleigh couldn't help but laugh at his exaggeration. She knew that the hood was talking about her if Scratch knew her business. "I'm doing real good, Scratch. I'm clean now, and I'm happy," she stated. She reached into her Birkin bag and pulled out her pocketbook. She peeled off three hundred-dollar bills. "Here you go, Scratch." She handed him the money. She knew how it was when you had a monkey on your back and you couldn't get it off. "Take care of yourself, okay."

Halleigh literally would have given Scratch the shirt off her back, and that was because they had a connection that was formed in the gutter—a bond similar to the one soldiers form with one another when they're in a foxhole and enemy armies are gunning at them, trying to kill them. She knew that Scratch would use the money to get high. And while she hoped that he would one day get help and get clean, she wasn't going to act holier-than-thou and forget where she'd come from. So, she helped him out with some of her blessings.

"Yeah, okay, Li'l Rina. You take care too," he

replied as he watched her walk into the building. "My Li'l Rina, my Li'l Rina," he mumbled. He was happy that the young girl was clean and healthy. Scratch smiled, thinking about how Halleigh's life had changed for the better, and about his next stop, the nearest dopeman to get his next fix.

Chapter Ten

Halleigh lay next to Malek. Her head rested on his chest, and their fingers intertwined as they sat back and enjoyed each other's company. It was the first time in a long time they had spent some quality time together. Lately, the only thing that Malek had time for was getting money. His constant hustling had caused her to spend many lonely nights in their new home.

"I've missed you," she whispered intimately.

"I know. I'm sorry I haven't been around much. You know what I've been doing. I've got to make sure that we want for nothing. A couple years of hustling and we'll be set for life. I'm doing this for us," he replied while he ran his fingers through her hair. He knew that he had been neglecting home, but it was for a good cause. He was making money in the hood, and he had to be on point if Halleigh wanted to continue to live the lavish lifestyle that he was providing for her.

"I know, I know," she said. "It still doesn't stop me from being lonely sometimes."

Malek noticed the disappointed look on her face and sighed deeply. "Look, Hal, I'm here now, ma. Let's just enjoy this time together, a'ight. It's all about you today."

"Okay," she reluctantly answered with a light smile.

Malek pulled his T-shirt over his head in one swift movement and then turned her on her back. He kissed her neck gently, running his warm tongue across her skin.

Halleigh arched her back in anticipated pleasure, but before she could get into it, Malek's cell phone rang loudly. "Don't answer it," she whispered with lust in her voice as she turned Malek's head back toward her.

Malek kissed her distractedly as the phone continued to ring. "Give me one minute," he said as he rose from the bed.

Halleigh sighed as she watched Malek walk over to the dresser to answer the phone. She knew that his focus could never be on her completely. The streets didn't allow it.

"Hello?" Malek said as he flipped open his cell.

"Yo, fam, I got that for you. I just picked up the scratch, and it ain't what it's supposed to be, nah mean?" Mitch was on the other end of the phone, and the news he was delivering wasn't good.

"What you mean, fam?" Malek asked. His workers had come short on his money last month, and after a routine shakedown, he was confident that it wouldn't happen again. This was becoming a problem.

"Shit's like a hunnid thou short," Mitch informed heatedly.

"A'ight, fam, come through my spot. We got to figure this shit out, and we also gotta talk about handlin' them niggas, Sweets and Manolo. If I don't respond soon, then the streets is gonna start thinking I went soft. You feel me?" Malek said.

"I'm about fifteen minutes away from your crib. I'll be there in a minute," Mitch replied.

Malek allowed Mitch to know where he lived, simply because he thought about how Jamaica Joe had operated, never even letting his closest henchman know where he officially rested. Malek understood why Joe did what he did, but at the same time, he reasoned that if the closest people in your organization didn't know where you lived, then that would breed mistrust in them and cause envy and hate to build up in your top people.

Malek snapped his cell phone closed and looked back toward the bed. Halleigh looked disappointed as she got up then walked out of the room, shaking her head. Malek let her leave. He didn't have time to entertain her. No matter how much he wanted her, he had other things that were more important at the moment. His workers were coming short with his money, and he needed to figure out why.

He put his cell phone on his clip and put on a white Enyce T-shirt before joining Halleigh in the kitchen. He found her standing in front of their liquor cabinet. She poured herself a glass of wine as he walked up behind her and wrapped his arms around her waist.

"You upset?" he asked her, already knowing the answer to his question.

"It's all about me today, huh?" she replied sarcastically as she sipped her red wine. She knew that she loved her man, but she was feeling left out of his life. He made sure that she was taken care of. Halleigh literally wanted for nothing, but the thing she craved the most was his presence. They had missed so much of each other's lives, and all she wanted to do was to make up for lost time. She wanted to get to know Malek again. Mentally they had grown, and physically they needed to become acquainted again.

"Don't be like that," Malek stated. "I love you, Halleigh. I just have to handle this, a'ight." He kissed the nape of her neck as she stood with her back toward him.

The feeling of his lips on her body sent shivers down her spine and left her vulnerable to his touch. She couldn't help but forgive him.

"Okay, Malek, but you need to make some time for me one of these days. She misses you too," Halleigh whispered erotically, referring to the yearning that she felt between her legs. She tugged at his earlobe with her teeth and slipped her tongue inside.

Malek's loins called for her. He picked her up by the waist, his hands firmly planted on her ass and her legs wrapped snugly around him, their

FLINT BOOK 4: RESURRECTION   103

tongues entangled. Malek placed her on the kitchen counter as he took a position between her legs. He could feel the intense heat coming from Halleigh's body. Her desire obvious, he suddenly forgot about his duty to the streets.

Ding-dong! The ringing of the doorbell interrupted their rendezvous.

Malek closed his eyes and rested his forehead against hers. "Hold that thought. We gon' finish this as soon as I'm done with business," he said.

"I hope so," she replied with a mischievous smile as she picked up her wine glass.

Malek went to answer the door and was greeted by Mitch. They slapped hands and embraced quickly before Malek invited him into his home.

Mitch looked around and was impressed by the interior of the expensively decorated living space. Malek was definitely doing well. "What up, fam?" Mitch asked as he took a seat on Malek's oversized leather sectional.

"This money, nah mean?" Malek replied, pacing back and forth. "What is up with these niggas? Them dudes you got out here playing wit' my money? I thought we already made an example out of Big Petey. Pour that on the table," Malek instructed, indicating the duffel bag full of money that sat at Mitch's feet.

Mitch unzipped the bag and emptied the contents onto the coffee table, covering it with wrinkled bills. They began to separate the bills by denomination, and when they were organized, they pulled out the money machine.

"What is this?" Malek asked as he looked at the bills going through the money machine.

"That's the take. That's what we made this week, fam," Mitch answered as he shook his head in disbelief.

Malek had noticed his paper was short in the Fifth Ward, usually his most profitable block for cocaine. For the past couple of weeks, he had begun to see his money decline in that neighborhood, and he began to grow suspicious.

Malek stopped the money machine and calmly sat back in his chair, shaking his head from side to side, obviously disturbed. *Either niggas is skimming off the top or crackheads just stopped smoking rocks. That is the only explanation for the Fifth Ward not to do numbers,* Malek thought as he looked over at Mitch. Malek had been hustling with Mitch for months, and Mitch hadn't shown any sign of disloyalty up to that point.

"Why is the paper constantly coming short from the Fifth, Mitch?" Malek folded both of his hands and leaned back in his seat.

"Niggas saying it's hard to eat because of that new rehabilitation center that was built on Detroit Street. They built it right in the middle of the hood. They be having bullhorns and shit, protesting with signs. No one want to be making their pay in that kind of environment. Feel me?" Mitch answered.

"Man, one rehab ain't shutting down an entire block—someone is putting they hand in the cookie jar," Malek stated.

"Nah, they ain't stupid. They ain't tryin'-a see us. We just got product that ain't moving. I got workers that usually move three bricks a week sitting on 'em 'cause they can't get 'em off like usual because of that center, fam," Mitch explained.

"What's the rehabilitation center called?" Malek asked, confused.

"Um . . . The—"Mitch snapped his fingers, trying to remember the name of the place, and it finally came to him—"The Genesis, yeah, that's what the shit's called. Some reformed addict named Moses is in charge of it."

The Fifth Ward was the source of about half of Malek's drug income, so this was definitely a problem.

"How can a little-ass center stop us from making money?"

"It's just hard trying to sell drugs while someone is on a bullhorn telling people that it will eventually kill you. Li'l man that works for us said that half of his former customers are in their rehab. It's going to be impossible to do numbers while that center is there. They on some save-the-world shit, and it's costing us money."

"I mean, damn, you talking like everyone done stopped smoking. They still tryin'a get high," Malek said.

"Look, fam, that ain't the only problem," Mitch stated. "That faggot Sweets been causing problems on the South End too."

"Word is bond, Mitch. It's time to lay him down! How we gon' get at that homo-ass Sweets?" Malek asked in irritation. His tone indicated that he was obviously upset about the sudden change in profits, and even more so about Sweets and his annoying tactics.

"Man, Sweets can get got, and I know just how to get at his ass. According to the dudes we got posted on the South Side, Sweets been sending them young murderers he got to get his blocks back. You know Sweets be on that gay shit. Supposedly, he done already made an example out of a couple of our workers. They ain't trying to see Sweets like that, so they'll rather come short on our money than face him."

Malek was enraged. There was no way he was going to give up the South Side. He would rather go out in a blaze of gunfire than let Sweets kill his former boss and then muscle in on his territory. Malek was the first hustler to take control of both sides of the city, and Sweets wasn't going to stand in the way of his reign of power.

"We got to get rid of Sweets. I ain't tryin'a do this back-and-forth shit either, fam. I want him dead, nah mean?"

"Yeah, I hear you, fam. You know I'm with it, but that still don't handle our other problem," Mitch stated. He turned on the television and flicked to the evening news. "This rehab been all over the TV. They trying to expand and everything. You think it's a problem now, wait until they spread those centers all over the damn city."

Malek focused his attention on the screen and listened to the news report:

"Here in Flint, the drug problem has plagued our city for over a decade. For the first time in years, a rehabilitation center has been able to reach out to those citizens who struggle with drug addictions. Genesis opened just thirty days ago, and with limited funding has been able to reach out to our city. Genesis offers drug rehabilitation programs that promise security once the program is completed. They have job placement agencies, and even hand out weekly stipends to their patients. Upon completion of the program, the participants are given a check for the stipends that they have earned, and are helped to find residence and employment.

The organization was founded by none other than a woman who goes by one name: Moses. Moses is a reformed heroin addict and has been clean for more than twenty years. She has applied for federal funding, and the center is currently undergoing evaluation to see if it qualifies. The center has its first awards ceremony in exactly one week. The public is welcome to attend."

Malek hit mute on the remote control and shook his head. He couldn't believe that one rehab center was affecting his cash flow. There was never money to open up a rehab facility in the city, and now all of a sudden this one was sent from heaven, or some miracle shit, and now it was healing more addicts than Jesus.

"What the fuck, fam? This one place got all the addicts going clean?" Malek asked in frustration.

Mitch nodded his head and responded, "Not all

of 'em, but enough of 'em for us to feel it. Moses is relentless. She be coming onto the block to recruit the addicts. She even offers to reform the drug dealers. She's a problem, and if she gets that federal grant, she's going to really mess up our money."

"A'ight, a'ight," Malek stated as he sighed deeply. "We're about to settle this shit with Sweets. Then we'll focus on that center. Maybe we can convince them to relocate," Malek said as he pulled out his pistol and set in on the table.

Without Malek saying anything else, Mitch got the picture.

"Listen, there's this hoe-ass trick that I know, and she be fucking with Manolo, so I know we can get at him and Sweets through her," Mitch stated. He was referring to Keesha, but he didn't let Malek know who he was talking about, simply because he didn't fully trust Keesha and he knew that Malek had no love for her after she had whupped his girl's ass.

Malek didn't know it, but Mitch was doing a "Donnie Brasco" on him—He was playing both sides of the fence, and he was also a switch-hitter, down with that homo-thug shit. Right after Joe was murdered, Sweets had convinced Mitch to fuck with him, and they had a plan to not only divvy up the streets of Flint, but to also take over all of Detroit and split that down the middle as well. So although Mitch was telling Malek that the reason for the decline in money was due to the rehab center, he was just blowing smoke up Malek's ass. The real deal was that Mitch was robbing Malek blind.

Halleigh came walking through the living room on her way to her bedroom.

"Halleigh, come over here and meet my man," Malek called out to her as he outstretched his arm for her to take her place within his embrace. She wore pink pajama shorts and a matching wife-beater.

She walked over toward the men, but Malek blocked her view of Mitch.

"Halleigh, this is my man, Mitch. Mitch, this is Halleigh," Malek introduced as he wrapped his arm around Halleigh's shoulders.

Halleigh looked down at the man sitting on her couch and immediately recognized him. She felt as if she would lose the contents of her stomach, and her breaths became shallow as she stared at Mitch. The look in his eyes let her know that he knew who she was.

"I—it—it's nice to meet you," Halleigh said as she held out her hand.

Mitch, of course, knew exactly who Halleigh was. Keesha had been trying her hardest to describe her to Mitch, and when he saw the clip on the news of her getting her ass beat at the Pistons game, he immediately remembered paying to fuck Halleigh in the backseat of his car in the park on the day that Malek was shot.

He grabbed her hand gently and caressed it slightly. He wasn't going to bust her out, but he smiled and replied, "It's nice to meet you too, ma." He held her hand a little longer than needed, and she pulled it back to avoid Malek's suspicion.

Halleigh couldn't help but notice how good Mitch looked in his butter Timberlands, Sean John jeans and button-up shirt. His caramel complexion looked good enough to eat. But then she felt disgusted with herself for even feeling the tiniest bit of attraction to him, and so she averted her eyes to the floor.

Malek looked at her and peeped her nervous energy. "What you nervous for?"

Halleigh looked up at him, her mouth still dropped down in an *O* of surprise. "I'm not," she replied. "I'll be in the room." She slipped from underneath his arms and high-tailed her ass out of the room.

Mitch's eyes discreetly followed Halleigh out of the room. He definitely remembered her tight-ass virgin pussy, and he knew that the only thing tighter than that was a nigga's asshole. She had the best pussy he'd ever had, and hoped that they would cross paths again. Now he was seeing her on the arm of his man.

He looked up at Malek and stood to his feet. "I'ma get out of here, fam," he stated.

"A'ight, I'll get at you tomorrow, so we can get on that Sweets situation," Malek replied as he slapped hands with his boy. He walked Mitch to the door and sighed when he thought of all the problems that had suddenly arisen. He definitely had a lot to deal with, and he didn't have a lot of time to do it.

Halleigh couldn't believe that Mitch was Malek's right-hand man. She couldn't believe that she had run into him again. Her heart racing nervously, she contemplated what she should do. Should she keep her mouth shut, or should she tell Malek what the deal was? He had been the first trick she had turned, and she remembered it as if it were yesterday. Her mind drifted back two years earlier, to the day she'd met him. . . .

"Ayo, ma, where you going?" a dude asked her as she walked by him. He was standing with his arms folded across his chest and a white bath towel draped over his head to shield his face from the hot sun.

Halleigh smiled as she continued to maneuver her way past them. The guy and all of his friends watched her backside as the natural sway of her hips commanded their attention.

Mimi stopped in mid-step, causing Halleigh to bump into her. Mimi looked at her like she was crazy.

"What?" Halleigh asked.

"Girl, you better go back over there and make that money," Mimi stated. She glanced back at the group of dudes. "I'm trying to get down too. Them niggas is crazy paid. So go on and hook it up." Mimi gave her a light shove.

Halleigh strutted back over to the group of dudes. "You checking for me?" she asked the guy that had called out to her.

He grabbed her hand and held it above her head as he watched her step in a full circle, her juicy ass cheeks shifting from side to side as she turned around.

"What's your name, ma?"

Before Halleigh could respond, Mimi cut in, "What's your government? You all into my girl shit. How about you let her know who you are and what you're about. Then she'll decide if you worth fucking with." Mimi was arrogant and smart-mouthed, but her looks allowed her to be.

The dude smiled and rubbed his goatee as he looked at the two young girls in front of him. He figured they had to be only 17 or 18. He was 26, but he loved young pussy. "Chill, shorty. I'm Mitch," he stated.

"Well, what's up? What you working with?" Mimi asked, her arched eyebrows raised in suspense.

"Damn! What are you, her pimp or something? Can I kick it to your girl for a minute?" he asked politely, though irritated.

"Do you, baby. All I'm saying is, time is money, ya feel me?" she replied as she rubbed her fingers together as if she were flipping through bills.

"For real? Y'all getting down like that? You mean all I got to do is pay for this pussy?" he asked in disbelief as he stared at Halleigh.

Halleigh's heart was beating out of her chest.

Mimi nudged her. "That's all it takes," she responded in an embarrassed whisper.

"Shit, take a walk with me then, shorty," he said as he grabbed her hand.

Before she walked away, Mimi grabbed her hand and whispered, "Get the money first."

Halleigh nodded, and then she followed him to a '07 Cadillac Deville.

He opened the door for her. "Get in," he stated.

"*You got the cash?*" *she asked, nervously looking around.*

"*How much you taxing?*" *he asked. He couldn't believe that the gorgeous young girl in front of him was tricking.*

How much am I supposed to charge this nigga? *she thought.* "Two fifty," *she stated, hoping that she didn't short-change herself.*

He pulled out three hundred-dollar bills and handed them to her. She got into the car and felt her chest heave up and down as the small space became hot. Her hands began to sweat when she felt Mitch put his tongue on her neck.

"*Come here, ma. Why you all over there?*" *he asked as he pulled out his manhood.*

Just do it. Close your eyes and do what you got to do, *she thought as she unbuttoned her shorts and eased out of them. She straddled him and grinded her hips as he touched her breasts, squeezing them a little bit too hard.*

He slid her thong to the side, pulled out a condom, and slid it onto his throbbing dick.

Halleigh looked down at it. He was a decent size. He wasn't any bigger than Manolo, and she was grateful, because she didn't want it to hurt. She felt as if she were selling her soul to the devil when he put himself inside of her.

"*Shit, ma, you a virgin?*" *he asked when he felt her tight walls. She gripped him, and he loved the way the inside of her felt.*

A tear fell from her eyes as she stared out of the rear windshield and rode his dick at the same time.

"Damn, ma, you working it. Umm," he stated as she performed her new job.

Halleigh couldn't stop the tears from rolling down her eyes. I can't believe I'm doing this, *she thought.*

When he finally came, she got off of him, wiped her eyes, put her shorts back on, and quickly exited the vehicle.

Halleigh snapped back into reality when Malek entered the room.

Malek could see the look on Halleigh's face and frowned. "You good?" he asked.

Halleigh knew that she must have been wearing her heart on her sleeve. Malek could always tell when something was on her mind. "Yeah, I'm good."

Malek climbed into the bed beside her and massaged her back. The feelings of his hand on her body caused moisture to form between her legs. She was yearning for him and couldn't wait to have him inside of her.

Sex had always been equated to money with her. For the first time ever, she was intimate with a man, and it was her choice to give herself to him.

Malek looked into her eyes as he slipped two fingers into her opening, which was now dripping wet. Their faces were so close that they could feel each other's breath.

"I'm sorry for everything," Halleigh whispered. She began to grind her hips as he fingered her.

"Shh!" he whispered. "You don't have anything to be sorry about."

Malek had no idea that Halleigh was actually apologizing for having had sex with Mitch, his new right-hand man. He showered her body with kisses, beginning at her neck and making a trail down. His tongue caressed her erect nipples, and he tugged on them softly with his thick lips.

A moan escaped her lips as he continued to go south. He lifted her hips and lowered his head, French-kissing her middle. He gave her clit attention that she'd never experienced, causing her to scream out in pleasure. His mouth was warm, and the heat felt good on her swollen jewel. She began to grind against his face, her legs spreading wider as she came over and over again.

Malek's manhood hardened, and his nine inches grew. Halleigh's moans only intensified his hunger for her. His penis throbbed and pre-cum rested on the tip. He explored her lips with the tip of his dick, and the sensation of the wetness caused him to call out. "Shit," he whispered as he eased himself into her.

Halleigh tensed up out of habit. She'd learned to fear sex. Being forced to prostitute herself had given her a misconception of sex. She held her breath when Malek entered her.

He looked down at her. Again, there were tears in her eyes. "Are you sure you want to do this?" he asked.

She nodded. "Yes, I'm okay. Make love to me."

"I would never hurt you, Halleigh," he whispered as he rocked inside of her. He maneuvered in and out of her, catching a slow rhythm as he thrust passionately. He felt her body relax beneath him, and she matched his pumps intensely.

Malek's manhood was thick, and it stretched her walls as he brought her pleasure. Sweat glistening on his chest, he leaned into her and kissed her on the lips.

Halleigh moaned loudly as he deep-stroked her. She had been fucked before, but never had she felt the intense emotion that was connected to her love-making with Malek.

Halleigh's toes began to curl, and her face twisted in contortion as she felt herself climaxing. "Malek!" she called out as her back arched. "What are you doing to me?"

"Loving you," he whispered as he watched her cum. The look on her face caused him to pump faster and deeper.

As the bed rocked and the headboard hit the wall, Halleigh could feel his manhood throbbing as he let off his seed inside of her, collapsing on top of her and kissing her forehead.

"I love you," he told her.

"I love you, Malek," she replied as she nestled in his arm and fell into a comfortable sleep.

Mitch couldn't believe that he had run into Halleigh again. After he fucked her, he had thought about her for weeks. He had even contacted

Manolo to see how he could have her. But Manolo wasn't a fool. He knew that Halleigh was a hot commodity and wasn't to be sold.

When he saw her tonight, Mitch was happy that she had managed to stop selling her pussy. Although Manolo was his man, Mitch knew instinctively that Halleigh never should have been selling pussy because she was a good girl and wasn't built for that shit.

But he was saddened by the fact that Malek had gotten to her first. Halleigh was perfect. Her beauty was uncanny. He wouldn't hesitate to fuck her again if he got the chance. And, in fact, he was definitely gonna go after her as soon as Sweets bodied her man Malek. Mitch wouldn't violate his man by coming at her, but if Malek ever fucked up, he would make sure to be there to pick up the pieces.

Chapter Eleven

Malek and Mitch sat in front of Big Al's, a local soul food spot. They had just ordered some food and were plotting on Sweets as they sat in the car and picked at their fried catfish dinners. They both had automatic pistols sitting in their laps and ski masks in the backseat. They had been staking out Sweets' house for hours, waiting for him to show his face. After seven hours of stalking, their hunger got the better of them, and they decided to call it a night.

"You sure you trust that bitch? This is the crib, right?"

"Fam, I got this! Shorty wouldn't do me dirty. Let's bounce, but we gon' get this nigga. Trust me on this," Mitch said.

Malek put his food back in the bag and started his car. He looked in his rearview mirror to observe the block. A few minutes passed as they continued to pick at their food, and just as they were about to drive away, a white Denali pulled into the parking lot. Sweets exited the car, and an entourage of killers followed him into the restaurant. It was obvious that Malek and Mitch would be outnumbered if they approached Sweets on some beef shit.

"Ain't this about a bitch? We've been trying to catch up with this nigga all day and here he is," Mitch stated in mock disbelief, knowing that all the time that they had spent staking out Sweets' crib had been just a front on his part. He had known all along that Sweets wasn't home and that he wouldn't be home all day.

"We can't just rush up in there," Malek stated more to himself than to Mitch. His mind was turning as he tried to devise a plan to get at Sweets. Murder was his motivation, and he wanted nothing more than to avenge Jamaica Joe's death. He knew that if he took an attempt on Sweets' life and failed, it would spark a bloody assault, if not an all-out blood bath, on his soldiers in the street. If Malek was gonna make a move on Sweets, he knew that he had to hit him and kill him. He couldn't take a shot at him and miss or simply wound him. Anything less than killing Sweets would further fuck up his money, so he had to put his anger aside and think strategically for a solution that was beneficial to everyone. Even if it meant giving Sweets a temporary pass.

"I know. He got them Shotta Boy niggas with him, and you know they stay strapped. We can't roll up in there with two pistols against all that," Mitch said. He was referring to two of the Shotta Boyz, a group of blood brothers who were trained to be killers from the time that they'd learned to walk.

"Fuck it!" Malek stated. "I'ma give Sweets a chance to save his own life. It's like I told you: a war keep everybody's pockets on *E*. I'll let Sweets have the South Side back if I'm getting forty percent of the take and if he cops his weight from me." Malek said that to test Mitch's response.

"You think he gon' go for that?" Mitch asked.

Wrong response, Malek thought.

He knew that if Mitch was really gangsta and riding with him, he would have been in fight mode and wouldn't want to be diplomatic about shit. Now Malek had to question just what was up with Mitch.

"Yo, fam, what was the chick's name who put you on to where Sweets rests at?"

Malek's question caught Mitch off guard.

"Eh? Oh, oh, Monica. The chick's name is Monica. She used to fuck with Sweets real heavy."

"Fuck with him like how?" Malek asked.

Mitch didn't answer the question. Instead he tried to change the subject back to what Malek had mentioned just a few minutes ago. "So, yo, you really think he gon' go for that deal?" Mitch asked again.

Malek didn't press Mitch on the name of the chick, but he knew right then and there that Mitch more than likely had been bullshitting him the whole time. He played along with it. "He ain't gon' have a choice. He can either take these bullets courtesy of Jamaica Joe or fall in line," Malek replied. He got out of the car and walked across the darkened parking lot.

Mitch reluctantly followed him. He knew that he could be walking into a potential death trap. If Sweets saw him with Malek, he would wonder if Mitch was really down with Malek. So Mitch strategically kept his hand on the handle of his chrome pistol as they headed into the restaurant.

Malek's adrenaline was pumping, and he could hear his heart beating in his ears. Malek walked in, and the bell above the door rang, causing Sweets and his entourage to turn around.

Sweets' face turned up in disgust at the sight of Malek. He pulled the red Blow Pop from his mouth as he placed his hand near his waist.

Mitch nodded to Sweets, to let him know that everything was straight.

"Look at this muthafucka," Sweets said with a smirk, "living in Jamaica Joe's shadow and trying to run my side of town."

The sound of Joe's name coming from Sweets' lips sent rage through Malek's heart. "You might wanna keep my man's name out your mouth, nah mean?"

The Shotta Boyz sent glaring stares his way, and Malek sent them right back.

"You lucky I'm not coming in here to twist your shit back behind that stunt you pulled at the Pistons game, but I'm about my bidness," Malek said. "I hear that you're interested in getting your hood back."

"I never lost my hood, fam," Sweets replied with larceny in his heart. "Can't you tell? I mean, considering how you a businessman and all, ain't you curious why your money been so short lately?" Sweets winked at Malek and blew him a seductive kiss.

"See, I've got a problem with that 'cause them streets belong to me now. Ain't no North Side-South Side beef, 'cause all that paper coming to me. Now we can blaze out for them blocks if you want to—" Malek pulled his nine out of his waist and let it rest in his hand by his side as he continued. Sweets saw the move and removed his pistol as well—"But you and I both know that wouldn't be a good thing. If we out here killing each other, we ain't making no money. Don't nobody like to watch over they back every minute, nah mean?"

Sweets wasn't a fool. He could see that Malek was setting up some sort of negotiation. He wasn't against that, but the way he saw it, Malek had to really sweeten the pot. Otherwise, Sweets would be shorting himself, especially since he was already getting a piece of Malek's money through Mitch.

"So what's up? Speak to me, young'un," Sweets said.

"I'll give you your blocks back under two conditions," Malek said. "One, you cop your work from me, and two, you give me forty percent of your profit." Malek could see the anger behind Sweets' eyes.

"You must think it's a game, young'un. I run those blocks on the South—"

Before Sweets could finish his sentence, Malek raised his pistol and fired a shot into one of the goons standing behind Sweets.

Sweets' and Lynch's eyes bugged in anger. Lynch, the only remaining Shotta Boy, knew that he should've carried his pistol into the restaurant. Now he was naked and vulnerable, and they had no choice but to agree to Malek's terms.

"Uh-uh. Keep them hands up, baby," Mitch said as he waved his gun back and forth between Sweets and Lynch.

"Like I said, we can beef out, but if you want to live, you'll accept my offer," Malek added.

Sweets shook his head and laughed loudly. "A'ight, li'l nigga. You da man," he said in a mocking tone.

"Good."

Malek and Mitch backpedaled toward the door as they prepared to leave.

Before Malek was completely out of earshot, Sweets said, "Hey, Malek, how is your bitch doing?"

"What?" Malek asked, raising his voice.

Sweets snapped his fingers and said, "What's her name? Um, um . . . Halleigh, yeah, that's it."

Malek shook his head, knowing that Sweets had just made a threat on Halleigh's life. He walked out of the restaurant and ran to his car, where he pulled out of the parking lot, his tires screeching as he peeled off.

* * *

Scratch, fiending for a fix, looked at the garbage can where Malek's worker had hid his stash. There was nothing worse than being on *E* and not having any money. Scratch itched his arms as he schemed on the unsuspecting block hustler. He looked at the other fiend that stood beside him. They peeked around the corner, and their desperation caused them to devise a plan.

Scratch laid out the instructions to the woman he'd just met, and they agreed as they went about their get-high mission. "Okay, look," he said, "you go distract him with that ol' fish pussy you got, and Scratch will get the stash. Meet Scratch back in this alley, ya hear?"

Scratch watched with greed in his eyes as the raggedy-looking woman approached the young hustler on the block.

"Come on, daddy," she said, "let me get something. I'll give you something if you give me something." The woman dropped the dirty skirt and exposed her yellow- and brown-stained panties.

Scratched creeped up the block as the hustler responded.

"Bitch, get your ass out of here. If you ain't got the cash, you ain't got the coke," the hustler responded, keeping his hands in his pockets.

Scratch silently walked over to the trash can and picked up the bag of crack rocks.

Just then, the hustler turned around and noticed him. "Yo, you stealing my shit!" he screamed as he approached Scratch and snatched him up by his collar.

"Ah, nah, young'un, Scratch don't mean you no harm," Scratch explained nervously as he tried to shield his body from the hits of the young man.

The hustler raised his fist and brought it down over Scratch's face, causing his eyes to immediately swell.

"Aghh, man . . . wait!"

Scratch's cries didn't faze the hustler, but he was stopped by Halleigh's shouts as she ran up to the scene.

"Hey, what are you doing?" Halleigh screamed as she stepped out of her BMW. She was parked up the street from the busy salon when she saw Scratch getting jacked up on Malek's block. "Let him go!" she yelled as she stood back, her oversized Birkin bag hanging underneath her arm.

The hustler shoved Scratch away, out of respect for his boss' girl. He had never really seen Halleigh before, but he knew exactly who she was because of the car and expensive clothes that she sported.

Halleigh rushed over to Scratch and helped him up. His lip was busted, and he was bleeding as Halleigh led him to her car. "Are you okay?" she asked as she pulled away from the curb.

"Scratch is okay," he replied. "It take a whole lot more than some young'un to take me out the game."

Halleigh was worried. Scratch didn't look good,

and she could tell that he hadn't been eating well. "Scratch, are you hungry?" she asked.

"A little bit," he replied.

Halleigh knew that she was going to miss her scheduled hair appointment, but looking at Scratch, she could tell that he needed her. She drove to McDonald's and ordered Scratch some food. She watched as he scratched frantically at his arms, and tears came to her eyes. She knew how it felt to be "tweaking" and broke.

"Scratch, you're breaking my heart," she said. "I know this is you, but do you ever think about shaking this shit?"

"Scratch think about it all the time, Li'l Rina, but once you're on it, there is no turning back. I've been on this dope for over ten years. Dope runs through Scratch's veins more than blood," he explained.

Halleigh didn't reply as she watched him stuff the food into his mouth. She knew that he needed help, and she was determined to get him off the drugs. She didn't care how much he protested, he was going to get clean.

Halleigh rolled down her window as the stench from Scratch's body hit her nostrils. She tried her hardest not to frown up, but the smell was too much to tolerate. The stink from his body was permeating her leather seats, and she hoped that it wouldn't linger in her car after he was gone.

Scratch noticed Halleigh's twisted-up face and began to feel slightly embarrassed.

"It's okay, Li'l Rina. Where Scratch from, baths don't come easy. You can roll down ya winda. Scratch won't get offended." Scratch rolled down his own window and stared at the passing city.

Halleigh silently thanked God that Scratch let down his window, letting her off the hook. She released a forced smiled and tried not to hurt Scratch's feelings too much. "It's okay, Scratch," she lied. "I just got a bad headache, that's all."

"Where we going anyway, Li'l Rina?" Scratch asked as he patted down his raggedy Afro.

"Scratch, would you do anything for me?" Halleigh asked, obviously trying to avoid his question.

"What kind of question is that? You know Scratch will do anything fo' you, girl," Scratch said, displaying his brown, buttery teeth.

"Scratch, I want to help you get better. I'm taking you to a rehab to get you clean," Halleigh said as she pulled into the Genesis Rehabilitation Center.

Halleigh had heard Malek express his dislike for the rehab center, which he thought was helping to dry up his business. And she knew that wanting to take Scratch to the rehab center was sort of like sleeping with the enemy. But the way she looked at it, Malek would be good with or without the rehab center; Scratch, on the other hand, would be dead very soon if he didn't get his habit in check.

"Come on, Li'l Rina, I don't need help!" Scratch said, feeling slightly betrayed.

Halleigh put her car in park and placed her hand over Scratch's. "Look, Scratch, it might seem crazy, but you are the only family I got. I know we're not blood, but we family. You the only one who acted like they gave a damn about me when I was out in those streets. I don't want to see you like this anymore," Halleigh said, tears forming in her eyes.

Odd as it may seem, Scratch was like a father figure to her. He was the father that she'd never had.

Even though they'd smoked drugs together, Scratch always felt guilty and wanted to reject the high, but the monkey on his back was too heavy. He looked in Halleigh's eyes and could not help but surrender. Her big brown eyes got him every time. He noticed how much she resembled her mother, and his heart melted. He used to have a thing for Halleigh's mother before she got turned out on the drugs.

"Well, I guess, Li'l Rina," Scratch mumbled as he dropped his head. He didn't want to admit it, but he didn't like who he had become. Scratch was one of the biggest drug dealers in his day, but fell victim to his own product. Halleigh didn't know it, but she was Scratch's only family also. No one gave a damn about him, and for Halleigh to tell him that he was family meant the world to him.

"Yes!" Halleigh yelled as she hugged Scratch, disregarding the foul odor that reeked off of him. She felt obligated to help Scratch beat his addiction, like Tasha had helped her beat hers.

One of the most painful things she'd had to do was walk away from Tasha at Malek's request. Tasha had single-handedly gotten Halleigh off drugs, so she was grateful. She had no way of showing her gratitude to Tasha, so by helping Scratch get off drugs, it helped put her mind at ease. She looked at it as passing on the gift of unwavering concern that Tasha had shown her.

"But I ain't getting up in front of no folks talking about I'm a crackhead and all. I be seeing that on TV. Them folks make you get up and say what you did for a hit. I even saw a man say 'I sucked dick for crack.' He had to be outta his cotton-picking mind. Scratch might be a junkie, but I never pulled any gay shit to support my habit. Scratch love the ladies too much fo' that. Hey, I might be ugly, but in my day I woulda gave them a run fo' they money," Scratch boasted, poking his chest out and patting his Afro.

Halleigh smiled and admired how Scratch could look like he did, but somehow could charm a lady with a couple of sentences. She exited the car and walked hand and hand with Scratch into the building.

Scratch squirmed and tussled in his dorm's bed, as his body tried to separate him from its addiction. Suffering from the worst of both worlds, Scratch was addicted to heroin and crack cocaine. Drenched in his own sweat, he clenched his aching stomach. The lack of heroin in his system caused his body to undergo complete agony.

The counselors offered Scratch methadone to help him wean himself off the drug, but he refused. He wanted to beat his addition cold turkey. He wasn't trying to shake his heroin addiction just to become addicted to methadone. No. He was going to shake it on his own.

Scratch stood up out of the bed and began to pace the room in attempt to ease the pain in his stomach muscles. Even his footsteps against the concrete floor sent pain through his body. The drug was calling for him.

"Come on, Scratch!" he said to himself as he frantically paced the small room. It took all of his might not to storm out of the rehab and hit the streets in search of a fix. The thought of Halleigh appeared in his head, and it crushed all desire to relapse. For years no one had shown that they cared for Scratch, but when Halleigh showed concern, he totally appreciated it.

"Scratch finally got someone in his corner!" he said, talking in third person as he always did. He balled up on the ground and clenched his aching stomach and cried himself to sleep. Scratch was taking this battle head on.

Scratch stood up in front of the group of fellow drug users. "Hello, " he said. "My name is Marcus 'Scratch' Pipes, and I'm a mu'fuckin' crackhead."

The room burst into laughter at Scratch's brutal honesty. Halleigh smiled as she saw Scratch trying to better himself. She sat toward the back and just watched as he testified in front of the small group.

Scratch continued, "I'm forty-two years old, and I've been smoking, shooting dope, stealing, and robbing for the past ten years."

Halleigh wasn't supposed to be in the meeting, but the rehab center agreed to let her sit in just that one time, since it was the only way Scratch would have gone through with the process. The rehab center had to also first make sure that it was okay with the other addicts.

The mediator, Moses, said as she sat in the middle of the group, "The first step to recovery is admitting you have a problem. Marcus has done that. Please give him a hand."

"Uh, no disrespect, baby, but could you please call me Scratch? Crackheads do have dignity, ya know. I don't want everybody to know my government name, baby," Scratch said smoothly before sitting back down and crossing his legs. Even though Scratch dressed in shabby clothes and smelled like ass, he had a certain swagger about himself. You could tell that he was somebody in his heyday. He looked back at Halleigh, who smiled at him, and he winked his eye at her.

Halleigh smiled back and took a glance at her watch. "Oh shit!" she whispered as she realized that she was late for her lunch with Malek. She quickly gathered her purse and slipped out the door. She put on her oversized shades and discreetly slipped into the brand-new BMW Malek had purchased for her.

She knew she was playing with fire, being on one of Malek's blocks. She wanted to tell him about helping Scratch, but she had promised him that she would stay out of the hood for all reasons and leave her former life behind. She didn't want to disappoint him, so she kept it a secret. After she made sure Scratch was good, she would never step foot in her old neighborhood again.

Halleigh maneuvered her luxury car through the city streets, trying to rush to the Italian restaurant to meet Malek.

Attorney Hill walked into the Genesis Rehabilitation Center with an Armani two-piece suit on, carrying a briefcase. He stuck out like a sore thumb amongst all the addicts and counselors. Malek had sent him to give the president of the rehabilitation center an offer she couldn't refuse. Hill approached the front counter and set his briefcase on the desk.

"Hello, I would like to speak with the owner of this facility," he said with a smile.

"Just a minute. I'll get her for you." The receptionist picked up the phone and notified Moses that she had a guest.

Moments later Moses came out of the back, her dreads neatly pulled away from her face. She greeted Mr. Hill with a smile and an extended hand.

Like a gentleman, Hill stood when she entered the room and shook her hand.

"Hello, I'm Martha. Everyone around here calls me Moses, though. How may I help you?"

"Jacob Hill. Nice to meet you. I'm here on behalf of my client. I would like to discuss a few things with you."

"No problem. Follow me into my office," Moses replied and waved for Hill to trail her.

Once they entered the office, Moses sat behind her desk and offered Hill a seat.

"That won't be necessary, ma'am." Hill set his briefcase on the desk and popped it open. "I've researched the worth of this property. Since this is a non-profit organization, the revenue isn't that great. So, I say you gross about thirty thousand a year from the federal grants, correct?" Hill asked.

"Yeah, that's about right. What are you getting to?" she asked as a confused look formed on her face.

Hill turned the open briefcase toward Moses, revealing the stacks of Benjamin Franklins. Hill fixed his tie and smiled slyly. "My client wants to offer you one hundred thousand dollars. You see, he wants this establishment to close down immediately."

Moses closed the briefcase and gently pushed it toward Hill. She couldn't believe her eyes. She looked up at Hill in puzzlement. "I know what you getting to, Mr. Hill. This won't be necessary. Genesis wasn't established to be a profitable organization. We're here to clean up our community and help with the increasing drug use that's killing our residents."

"I thought you might say that. My client would like to offer you two hundred thousand dollars, double the amount."

"What are you trying to do, Mr. Hill? We are not going anywhere. You must work for a drug dealer.

I can't stand people like you. You come in here with your fancy suit and blinging cuff links, trying to push people like me out of the community so you can continue to poison it. You can tell your client that I said no thank you," Moses said as she walked to her door and opened it. "Have a good day, Mr. Hill."

Hill closed up the briefcase and proceeded out of the door.

"Good day," Hill said as he exited the office.

Moses didn't know what she had just gotten herself into. Whether she liked it or not, that neighborhood belonged to Malek Johnson.

Chapter Twelve

Ever since Sweets had made that "girlfriend" remark, Malek was concerned for Halleigh's safety and was keeping constant tabs on her. He called Halleigh's cell phone and didn't receive an answer. He hadn't heard anything from Sweets, but the threat that he had made was still fresh in his mind. Yeah, he had been paranoid since seeing Sweets, and the fact that Halleigh wasn't answering her phone only irritated him more. His money had still been coming short, and as the rehab center grew more popular, his pockets grew shorter and shorter.

Malek had plenty of money saved up, but he wasn't ready to let go of the game. He loved the power and respect that he received in the hood. He was a boss, and he was going to hold on to that status until he no longer could.

His lawyer had called and informed him that Moses had denied his proposition, so he knew that he had to approach the situation differently. He was going to go to plan B. If Moses wouldn't leave his hood willingly, he would make her.

Halleigh sent Malek to voice mail for the third time. She hated ignoring his calls, but if he knew that she was in the inner city, he would trip on her. She couldn't handle his questions right now. She just wanted to help Scratch, and she knew that Malek would never understand why.

When Halleigh walked into the clinic, Moses greeted her with open arms. "Welcome, Halleigh," she said. "It's so good of you to come here as often as you do to check on your friend."

"It's really not a problem. I just want to support him. I know how hard this is, and I'm proud of him for trying."

As Moses nodded, her medium-length dreads, bounced up and down. She was the kindest woman that Halleigh had ever met, and Halleigh would've never guessed that the woman had once been strung out on drugs.

"Well, his body is still detoxifying itself. He's in a lot of pain, so be sure not to touch him."

Halleigh nodded and then made her way back to Scratch's room. She sat with him as he shook and trembled. He looked so weak, and seeing him like that reminded Halleigh of her own experience. Tasha had taken good care of her. She was there for Halleigh and had been such a good friend, and Halleigh missed her dearly.

She sat with Scratch for an hour and promised to come back later that week.

"Take care," she said when she left. She looked at her phone and noticed that she had two more missed calls from Malek. She knew that she would have to come up with a good excuse because he was going to want to know where she was.

When she walked into her house, Malek and Mitch were sitting in her living room. Both men looked up at her, and she could see the worried expressions on their faces.

"Where you've been?" Malek questioned. "I've been blowing your cell up all day."

"I was at the mall." She felt bad for lying to him, but she couldn't tell him the truth.

"When I call you, answer the phone!" Malek yelled as he pointed his index finger in her face.

"Okay, Malek, damn it! You don't have to yell at me." It was the first time that Halleigh had seen him display that kind of aggression toward her, and tears came to her eyes.

"I'm sorry. I didn't hear you call. I probably didn't get service in the mall," she added, hoping that he believed her story. The last thing that she wanted was for him to become suspicious of her and think that she was cheating.

"You heard what I said!" He grabbed his car keys and put on his fitted hat. "Keep your ass in the house until I get back," he said as he walked out of the house.

Mitch rose from the couch. As he walked past Halleigh, he could see that she was on the verge of tears. He wiped away a single tear that had trickled down her face, and she tensed up from his touch.

"When that nigga fuck up, you got somewhere to go," he whispered in her ear.

Halleigh knew what he was getting at. She could tell that he was feeling her, but this was the first time he had verbalized his interest. Every time she was around him, she felt awkward, but she couldn't see herself jeopardizing her relationship with Malek to be with him. She turned her head to the side and walked to her bedroom as Mitch let himself out of the house.

Mitch had been spending a lot of time at Malek's crib, since the two of them were constantly talking business and trying to make sure that everything was straight. And ever since the second time that he had come over to the house, he would flirt with Halleigh with every opportunity that presented itself.

Halleigh thought back to the second time that Mitch had come over to the crib with Malek and what had transpired when Malek went to the basement of the house to use the bathroom.

Mitch spoke in a low, seductive tone as he moved in close to Halleigh. "That pussy still tight?"

Halleigh's heart began to beat from fear of what Malek would do if he walked in the room and saw Mitch all up on her. "Mitch, what are you doing?" Halleigh said through gritted teeth. "Back up off me!"

"You ain't tell Malek that we fucked, did you?"

Halleigh's heart sank to her feet. "Mitch, you are really bugging right now! Do you know Malek would murder you in a heartbeat if he heard what you just said? No, I didn't tell him!"

Mitch smiled and then leaned in and kissed Halleigh on her neck and said, "Good. Then we still got our little secret."

"Mitch! What is wrong with you?" Halleigh punched Mitch and pushed him off.

"My bad, my bad," Mitch said, smiling a devilish smile and then backing off Halleigh just as Malek re-entered the room.

Halleigh's stomach turned sour at the thought of Malek not knowing that she had been with Mitch, and at the thought of lying to him. She felt like she had to throw up and rushed into the bathroom as the contents of her stomach came up.

Afterward, she ran herself a bath and prepared herself for bed. She was extremely tired. She looked at the clock on the nightstand beside her bed. It was only eleven o'clock, so she knew that Malek wouldn't be home anytime soon. She picked up the phone and dialed his number, but Malek's phone sent her directly to voice mail.

Halleigh left a message saying, "I love you, Malek," and she retired for the night, but she felt a huge amount of guilt as she lay in the bed tossing and turning.

She felt like she had to come clean with Malek, so she called his cell phone right back. She was actually glad when he sent her to voice mail once again, but this time she left a longer message:

"Baby, I feel bad about something, and I just gotta come clean with it. But please promise me that you won't get upset. Okay, well, I know how you feel about the rehab center cutting into your business, and I just wanted to tell you that when you was calling my phone and you couldn't get me, that was because I was really with Scratch at the rehab, trying to get some help for him." Halleigh winced as she said those words, as if she were bracing to get slapped by Malek.

Then she added, "And, baby, there's something else that I wanted to tell you, but I have to tell you that in person. It's about Mitch, okay, baby. I love you. Be safe. Call me back."

Halleigh let out a huge sigh of relief, but she knew that she had to first wait for Malek's reaction before dropping the bomb on him that Mitch had fucked her. But at least she felt like she could turn off the TV and sleep in some peace.

Halleigh felt Malek crawl into the bed with her at around four o'clock in the morning. Her heart began to race. She was feeling nervous, not knowing whether Malek had listened to her voice mail. She still had no idea why he had tripped on her the way that he had. She didn't know what was up with him and Sweets, and she was wondering if he was just stressed about his business.

Malek realized that by loving Halleigh publicly,

he had exposed his weakness to those around him, and now Halleigh could be a potential target. Her back was against his chest as he held her tight. He didn't say anything; he didn't have to. She knew that he loved her.

Halleigh could feel his heart beating through his chest. Something inside of her glowed as she thought about Malek. She thought about all that she had been through and knew that she would do it all again, if that's what it took to find her way back into the arms of this man.

The next morning, Halleigh woke up with the same urge to hurl. Feeling nauseated, she lay in bed groaning from the horrible feeling.

"What's wrong?" Malek asked.

Halleigh realized that Malek must not have heard her message, so she decided to just not bring up the subject. "I don't know. I don't feel good at all."

"You need to go to the doctor so you can get checked out."

"I don't think it's that serious," Halleigh replied.

Malek sat up on his elbow and brushed Halleigh's hair out of her face. "Do it for me, a'ight. I just want to make sure everything's good with you, ma."

"Okay, but you're coming with me."

Halleigh's trip to the doctor revealed that she was four weeks pregnant. It was the happiest news of her life. Tears came to her eyes when the doctor told her.

She looked at Malek to see what he thought, but she had a hard time reading his emotions. "What are you thinking?" she asked.

Malek was silent for a minute, so she continued, "If you don't want me to have this baby, I won't." She let her tears fall at the thought of terminating her pregnancy, but she would do anything to keep Malek, and if he wasn't happy about their situation, she would have no choice but to change it.

"You're having my seed," Malek whispered in disbelief as if the news was just now hitting him. He placed one hand on her flat stomach. "I can't believe I'm about to be somebody's daddy."

"So you're not mad?" she asked.

"Hell no," he said. "You're having my baby. I didn't think it was possible for me to love you anymore than I already did, but I do because you are the mother of my child."

Malek thought about his mother. How he wished she was still alive to be able to see her soon-to-be-born grandchild. Then his thoughts went to having a little boy. He visualized teaching him how to play sports, how to mack hoes. A huge smile came across Malek's face. He was about to be a daddy. *Life is so beautiful,* he thought.

Malek left the doctor's office that day with a new inspiration for life. He was about to be a father. He and Halleigh had made a lifetime commitment. Through their child, they were about to bond forever.

With his new responsibility to consider, Malek was determined to get on his grind even harder because he was going to make sure his family was taken care of. And he wasn't going to let Sweets or Moses get in the way of his family's safety or financial security. He made a phone call on his way home.

Mitch answered on the first ring. "What's good, fam?"

"Have you heard anything about Sweets?"

"Nah, since that shit popped off at Big Al's, he's been laying low. Maybe he got the message," Mitch replied.

"For his sake, I hope so. I'm tying all loose ends. Hal is pregnant, and I need to get this money, nah mean?"

"Yeah, I hear you, fam."

"Ride out with me tomorrow, a'ight. It's time to take care of that rehab situation."

"No doubt," Mitch replied. He thought of the seed that was growing inside of Halleigh's womb and couldn't help but wish that she was his. "Congratulations, fam. Send Halleigh my love." He hung up the phone and tried to take his mind off Malek's woman.

Chapter Thirteen

Scratch sat through a lecture by a reformed drug addict and was proud of himself. He hadn't touched a drug in eight weeks. Today was the day he graduated from the twelve-step program. Scratch kept glancing at the door, waiting for Halleigh to walk in so that he could share his special day with her. She promised she would be here.

I know baby girl ain't gon' let Scratch down, he thought as he played with his fingers nervously. He thought of how he had wasted years of his life in the streets, being a menace to society. He thought about Halleigh coming to his rescue like she did. He wasn't used to anyone showing him any kind of concern, so it was a breath of fresh air to have someone in his corner.

As the motivational speaker spoke, Scratch saw something that almost made his heart stop. Sharina, Halleigh's mom, walked in. It had been years since he had last seen her, and she looked good. Scratch was so happy to see her. He had honestly thought that she was dead, that she'd suffered the same fate as many of his drug-addicted cronies.

The crackhead's glare that was in her eyes the last time he had seen her was now gone. She came in and sat in the back of the crowded room. He couldn't believe the resemblance she had to her daughter. Even at her mature age, she looked as if she could be Halleigh's sister.

Scratch was glad that he'd decided to shave that morning. Back in the day, he had a thing for Sharina, and clearly the attraction was still there. He sat up straight and patted his Afro, trying to look as presentable as possible.

"Yo, we outside of the building right now," Mitch said as he sat in the black Navigator with three of his goons. "We're just waiting for the go-ahead." They all had fully loaded semi-automatic assault rifles.

Malek was on the other end of the phone, watching as Halleigh pulled off to go to her doctor's appointment. "Is their kids there?" he asked, not wanting to hit any children.

"Nah, there aren't any children." Mitch took another glance to ensure that he was correct.

"Good. Wait until the majority of the people leave and do it. Hit it! We gotta send a message. They're fucking up the money," Malek said before he closed his cell phone and walked over to the couch. He didn't want to send a message that malicious, but Joe had taught him, when in the drug game, you had to be ruthless and detach all emotions from business.

Malek took a deep breath. He never thought that he would be ordering the shooting of a building full of innocent people, but to keep his position of power, he had to do it.

Halleigh rushed out of the house. She hated lying to Malek, but she had to be there for Scratch. He had finally completed the program, and she wanted to be there in his final steps to leading a clean life. She had even put some money up so that Scratch would be all right. She had managed to save five thousand dollars for him, trusting that he would do the right thing with the money.

Over the years she had grown to love Scratch. He had given her real advice during some of her toughest times, and she felt honored that she was able to repay him by helping him get clean, introducing him to a new life.

She glanced at her watch and noticed that she was late for Scratch's ceremony. She had promised him that she would be there to witness him receive his completion certificate from the drug program. *I'm so proud of Scratch for cleaning himself up*, Halleigh thought as she got in her car and headed toward Genesis.

*   *   *

Scratch's hands became sweaty as he approached Sharina, who was sitting in the back and listening attentively to the motivational speaker. It had been so long since he had seen her, and he wanted to reintroduce himself.

"Hey, beautiful lady," Scratch said.

Sharina looked at Scratch, and when she realized who he was, she looked like she'd seen a ghost. It had been years since she'd last seen him. "Oh my God," she said, placing her hand over her mouth.

Scratch leaned over and gave her a hug.

"Look at you, all cleaned up," Sharina said as she took a good look at Scratch. She had been in the streets a long time and could tell that Scratch hadn't been using.

They just stared at each other for a brief moment.

Sharina continued to look Scratch up and down. "How long have you been clean?"

"It's been eight weeks now," Scratch said proudly as he played with his fingers.

"I'm proud of you," Sharina said. She placed a gentle hand on Scratch's shoulder. "I know how hard it is to get the monkey off your back."

"Thanks. You looking good, Rina. I can tell by your eyes you're clean."

"Yeah, I have been clean about a year or so now," Sharina said confidently. "I had to get away from Flint for a while. I've been in Detroit for the past year. That's where I got my rehabilitation at.

Moses helped me out before she relocated down here. She invited me back to speak."

"Are you serious?"

"Yeah, I'm serious. I'm here to share my story with the group." Sharina's smile suddenly dropped, and she looked down before adding, "And I have some unfinished business."

"You talking about Halleigh, aren't you?" Scratch asked before he could catch himself. It just came out.

Sharina looked up with tears in her eyes. She was surprised to hear her daughter's name. It had been so long since she'd last seen Halleigh, and it ate at her daily. She had been preparing to come back to Flint to find her baby girl. She owed her so much explanation because of her bad drug problem. She had sold her daughter's virginity to the local dopeman just to feed her habit. She was ashamed, and she needed to find her daughter so that she could apologize. She knew that the words wouldn't mean much at first, but she was hoping that Halleigh would eventually forgive her.

Scratch smiled because Halleigh had promised him that she would show up for the program. He kept it to himself, so that Sharina would have a big surprise. *Scratch gon' make Rina's day*, he thought to himself as he stared at beautiful Sharina.

Halleigh couldn't stop smiling, knowing that she was about to bring a life into the world. She pulled into the parking lot of Genesis. *I hope I didn't miss seeing Scratch get his certificate,* she thought as her heels clicked on the pavement on her way into the building.

Halleigh walked into the building during the middle of a woman's speech and saw Scratch sitting in the front row. She immediately took a seat, so she wouldn't be a distraction. As she sat down, she heard a voice that she hadn't heard in years. She immediately looked at the podium, and anxiety took over her body. Standing there talking to the people was her mother. "Oh my God," she whispered as she sat there in disbelief.

"Drive by slow," Mitch instructed as he and another henchman, both with semi-automatic assault rifles, hung out of the window. The Genesis building had a glass front, so they could see all of the people gathered inside looking at the speaker. Under Malek's orders, Mitch prepared to let it rain bullets inside of the building.

"Thank you all very much," Sharina said as she received a standing ovation for her touching speech. She walked off the stage and over to Scratch and gave him a hug to congratulate him on his recovery.

Scratch whispered in her ear as they embraced, "I got someone I want you to see." Then he led her to Halleigh.

Sharina's heart nearly stopped when she saw her only daughter. She had been anticipating their reunion for so long, and now that she was face to face with her, she was speechless. She had so much to say, so much to explain, but nothing seemed to come out. Tears ran down her cheeks as she began to speak. "Halleigh, I—"

Before Sharina could finish her sentence, bullets rang out, one grazing her neck.

The entire place broke out into complete pandemonium. Scratch dove for Halleigh and covered her to protect her. The sound of shattering glass and horrified screams filled the air as they dropped to the floor, trying to avoid taking any bullets. After ten seconds of non-stop shooting, the mayhem finally ceased.

"Baby girl, are you okay?" Scratch asked as he uncovered Halleigh. He noticed blood coming from her thigh and panicked. "You hit! You hit in the leg!" he said as he looked at the rest of her body to make sure that she wasn't hit anywhere else.

A woman screamed, causing them to look in her direction. It was Moses. She had Sharina in her arms. Blood was coming from her neck, but fortunately for her, the bullet hadn't hit her jugular vein. It had merely broken her skin.

"Nooo!" Halleigh screamed as she scooted over next to her mother and held her in her arms. She didn't even get a chance to tell her how much she loved her, how much she hated her, how much she needed her, and how much she had to go through without her. She disregarded her own bullet wound as she asked her mom, "You okay?"

Thankfully, her mom wasn't dead, and she would eventually get a chance to tell her all of those things.

The sound of ambulance sirens sounded, and the paramedics rushed into the building to save the lives of the wounded.

Halleigh threw up, and the room began to spin, as she was losing an awful lot of blood from her leg. She looked down at her stomach, and for the first time she thought of the life inside of her. "Oh God, no, please no," she whispered. She put her hand over her wound and tried to stop the bleeding.

"You need to get to the hospital, Li'l Rina." Scratch waved a paramedic over to Halleigh.

Losing a lot of blood, Halleigh became lightheaded and fainted. The last thing that crossed her mind was Malek and her unborn child.

"It's done," Mitch said to Malek.

"Good. Maybe now they will see it my way." Malek hung up the phone.

Malek sat on the couch and looked at his watch. "Halleigh should have been home by now. Where my baby at?" he asked himself as he stood in his living room with a bottle of wine. The wind blew open his white linen shirt as he took a sip. He pulled out a box holding a three-carat diamond ring. That night was the night he would propose to Halleigh. *From here on out, life will be good.*

"Come on, girl, where you at?" Malek flipped open his phone and dialed her number, but he never received an answer. Malek checked his voice mail to see if Halleigh had left him any messages, and that was when he heard the message that she had left him the other night.

"Baby, I feel bad about something, and I just gotta come clean with it. But please promise me that you won't get upset. Okay, well, I know how you feel about the rehab center cutting into your business, and I just wanted to tell you that when you was calling my phone and you couldn't get me, that was because I was really with Scratch at the rehab, trying to get some help for him.

"And, baby, there's something else that I wanted to tell you, but I have to tell you that in person. It's about Mitch, okay, baby. I love you. Be safe. Call me back."

Malek quickly called back Halleigh's cell phone, but again he got no answer.

Immediately he thought the worst about Mitch. "I'll cut that nigga's dick off and shove that shit in his mouth and then murder his ass!" Malek screamed. He had a sick feeling as to what was up. "He snaked me! Don't nobody come in my crib and snake me and think they can live!"

All of the veins in Malek's head began to bulge, and fire was ready to shoot out of him. He took hold of his cell phone and called Mitch.

"Yo," Mitch said, answering his phone.

"Yo, Mitch, swing by the crib. I just wanna talk about this rehab shit, so all our bases is covered and nothing comes back to bite us in the ass."

"You want me to come right now?" Mitch asked.

"Yeah, yeah, and come solo. I ain't trusting nobody right now."

"Okay, no doubt. I'll be there in about a half-hour," Mitch said and then hung up the phone. He immediately got on the horn with Sweets. "It's time to roll on this nigga," he said to Sweets.

"A'ight, no doubt," Sweets said without hesitation. "Say no more. Swing by the crib. I'll line niggas up, and we'll get the ratchets and go tighten that ass up!"

Halleigh was slipping in and out of consciousness as she rode in the back of the ambulance. Scratch was right there by her side, tears in his eyes. "Come on, Li'l Rina, you'll be all right," he kept saying, hoping that she could stay conscious.

"She's lost a lot of blood!" one of the paramedics said as he tried to apply pressure to her wound.

Halleigh tried to whisper something, but Scratch couldn't make it out clearly. "What's that, baby girl?" Scratch asked, stroking her hair and placing his ear next to her lips.

Halleigh whispered, "My-my baby, my baby," just before losing consciousness. Those were the last words that she uttered, and she slipped into total darkness.

THE END
But the saga continues in *Flint 5*

Coming Soon in 2009

A Pimp's Life

By Treasure Hernandez

Prologue

My moms died today. The monster finally devoured her spirit and life. Sick the whole time through, she lived HIV-positive for fifteen years before finally succumbing to full-blown AIDS.

Drugs fucked up her whole shit up years ago. Fucked my whole shit up too. I watched her get high every day. It used to make me cry to see her after she hit that pipe. She'd be so lost in space. It was like her soul wasn't there, but her body was always there for anyone that could keep her high. I guess she finally reached that mountaintop she'd been climbing for so long.

What sense did it make though, when all she did

was fall off? Maybe my father could've given her a helping hand. If she knew who that was. She'd had a child with a man from Virginia three years before I was born. She never knew what it was, and didn't want to know, putting up the baby for adoption the instant it was born.

I may as well have been adopted too because I didn't like the idea of admitting that my moms was a crackhead ho. She didn't love me. All she ever loved was that pipe. You know how that shit makes me feel? It don't make me feel like nothing. Because if you ain't never known love, then you ain't going to miss love.

Chapter One

MACK

I shielded my eyes from the glare of the afternoon sun as I walked out of Queens Courthouse. It had been a long night. I'd just spent it serving nine hours behind bars, thanks to the brave and dedicated hard work of New York City's Finest. I walked down the long row of cement steps and stood at the curb. The traffic lights were out, and cars headed east and west, uncompromisingly whizzing by with no regard for pedestrians trying to make a dash for the island that divided the flow of traffic. I stood under the Don't Walk sign and pressed the button to no avail.

"Fuck it," I said, running into the street as soon

as I saw a momentary clearing. I jumped on top of the divider and looked to my immediate right. Cars raced up the street as if this was the "Ghetto 500." My heart pounded through my chest from running, and my adrenaline rushed like Russell's when he was up in that elevator catching the full force of a J.B. beat-down.

Soon as I hit the sidewalk my cell rang. "Yo," I said, panting heavily, searching for air.

"You get out yet, jailbird?" Sade laughed.

Sade was my woman. We lived together in a house in Queens Village. She wasn't the best-looking woman I'd dealt with, but she had a good heart. Sade was 5-6, and was dark-skinned with full lips like Fantasia. Originally from Virginia, she'd moved to New York three years ago after her stepfather, Glen, tried to rape her. When she brought the issue to her mom's attention, her mom flipped the script by accusing her of lying and trying to cause a rift in her stable relationship.

When Sade's moms finally did confront Glen with the charges, he denied it, swearing up and down every crack of ass he'd ever licked that Sade came on to him. Deep in her heart, she knew she was wrong, so she let her daughter go and moved right along. She knew Sade was telling the truth and that he'd always had his eyes on her. I mean, why not? Here you had this young woman physically blossoming right before your eyes versus a sickly, one-tittie lady, slowly but surely withering away.

Afraid of spending the latter years of her life

home alone, she chose his side, with her head down to the floor. That still bothered Sade to this day. She didn't understand how you could love somebody your entire life then just turn your back on them. None of the men her mother dated had good intentions.

Sade's moms was dying of breast cancer and had a huge life insurance policy. Every eligible bachelor in Richmond knew that she was worth four hundred thousand dollars after her ass expired. All she wanted to do was never die alone.

Sade would call her every now and again, but Glen always answered the phone and hung up when he heard her voice. Eventually he had the number changed, and Sade lost contact with her and refused to go visit her as long he was still living there.

"Yeah. I'm free. About to grab me some New York Fried Chicken from the Habeebs." I walked inside the restaurant. "Call Anton and tell him I said to come and get me. It's his fault I was in there in the first place," I said, sitting down. "Yo, Ahmed, let me get two thighs, small fries, and a lemon Mystic Iced Tea, man," I said to the owner. "Yeah, so, baby, did you miss me?"

"You know I did."

"Uh-huh. You better had."

"Whatever, Mack. I'm about to see the Dominicans. My hair needs to be washed and wrapped."

"Don't be out there spending up a whole lot of money, Sade. You heard?"

"Love you," she said, disconnecting the call.

*   *   *

I walked inside my Queens Village home and flopped down on the blue leather couch. I had been up the entire night madder than a mutha-fucka, sitting up in jail on some bullshit marijuana charge. I don't even smoke. My dude Anton was blowing one of them thangs down while we was inside Cambria Heights Park with these two bitches. I don't know which was faster, the detectives that rolled up in the park in the black Expedition with tinted windows, or Anton's warrant-having ass hopping over the five-foot gate at the end of the park. He dropped the cigar shit right in front of me. So guess who it belonged to, according to the law? They let the girls off with a warning and let me ride in back of the truck with them.

The doorbell rang just as I'd reached my comfort zone level. I ignored it at first, but the person continued to pound the fucking bell out. I looked through the peephole. "Ay, yo, who the fuck is it?"

Anton's big-ass head was all up in my view. I'm looking out the hole, his silly, non-complex ass is trying to look in.

"Open the door, man. You know I got warrants." He looked around before quickly rushing inside. Then he held out his hand. "Hey, man, apologies for last night."

"You's an ill dude, yo. I ain't fucking with you no more outside. I don't like being locked up. You just bounced without saying a word."

"If there was time to say anything, I would of. Look, I can't afford to get caught by these pigs, yo.

They'll kill me. That's what they do when you shoot one of theirs."

I walked to the refrigerator, pulled two Heinekens from the top shelf, and popped the caps. "Whatever, man. Did you ever speak to them girls in Brooklyn . . . Kim's people?"

"Aw, man, I was caught up in some next shit, son. But I'm-a get up with her tonight and shit. Matter of fact, you should come too. She keep asking about you."

"Naw. I'm chilling at home with Sade. I didn't get to give her no 'daddy good loving' last night because of your ass." I pointed at him.

Anton took a long swig of the beer. "Gordy was asking about you too."

"Yeah? I don't hear my phone ringing off the hook. He ain't looking for me. He looking for something about me."

"Well, whatever the fuck"—He held out his hand—"I'm about to be out. Just came to check in on you and make sure you wasn't violated in the shower." Anton laughed.

"Fuck you!" I laughed. "Get the hell out my house," I said, pushing him out and closing the door.

Chapter Two

MACK

"I'm thinking about taking a trip to see my mother." Sade sat up in the bed. She leaned her back against the headboard and touched my chest. "You heard me, baby?"

"Naw. What's up?" I said, my eyes still closed.

"I said I want to see my mother. What do you think about that?"

"Sade," I said, sitting up, "if you want to see your mother, I'll roll with you down there. It's nothing."

"No, I need to do this by myself. I'll be all right."

"What about ol' boy?"

"I'll worry about that when I get there."

"You sure?"

"I'm a big girl, baby. I'll be cool."

"A'ight. I know you can handle yourself. So when you leaving?"

"I'm driving down there next Friday. I'll be gone for about three days."

I kissed her cheek.

"What was that for?"

"For being a real thorough bitch. That's the shit right there that made me fall in love with you."

Sade reached her hand under the covers and placed it on my hardening dick, massaging the head with her thumb. "And that's the shit that made me fall in love with you," she said, removing the covers from over me. She pulled my boxers off and slowly slid her mouth around the head of my dick and sucked it like a swollen thumb, licking around the rim and poking at the eye with the tip of her tongue.

I lay on my back looking at her, as she widened her mouth and long-throated the nine inches of "bless you with my loving." She gagged once, she gagged twice, but maintained the sexual discipline required to control tossing it up. When my body shivered, she sucked even harder.

"AWWWW SHIIIIT," I yelled out. "SADE. Oh my damn," I cried out as she continued milking the cow.

"What's the matter, boo? You can't take it?" she asked, my love fluids leaking from the corners of her mouth. "Where the freak at, daddy?" She rolled her tongue around at me then stuck it down my throat.

I lifted off her shirt and sucked on her hard,

erect nipples, my mouth cruising around, on, and between her firm titties. I licked from her neck down to her navel and spoke to it in tongues. I melted down in between her legs and sniffed my pussy. And craved my pussy. I watched it as it throbbed and leaked in anticipation of a forth-coming tsunami.

"Come on, daddy, I wanna see lakes running down these sheets," she said, rubbing them with one hand while the other was snug behind my head.

I made her butterfly wings flap and her cat sing for tender victuals. I eloquently ran my tongue around the edges of each wing then quickly slid it further down. I pushed it up into her ass, and she sighed loudly. I razzled her and dazzled her with *tongue*nastic flips and twists, and turns and churns.

And then she farted in my fucking face. I was done.

"What happened, daddy?" Sade rubbed between her legs.

"Come on, man, how many times you going to fart in my face?"

She laughed. "Did it stink?"

"Oh, you think that shit is funny now, huh?" I playfully grabbed her by the shoulders and lay back down. "Come on, ma, get on top." I was standing strong as ever.

Wetter than a Mexican being rescued by the Coast Guard, Sade sat on it, and it slid straight up inside of her, the soft walls collapsing around me then constricting. As I lay still for a moment and let it burn, my body ushered in an even harder erection.

She planted her palms on my chest and slowly began to gyrate her hips a lil' something. She heard my black snake moan and matched it with a pleasurable meow. She leaned forward and grabbed my shoulders then began popping that thing up and down like hydraulics.

As we stared and growled at each other with the ferocity of a tiger and tigress, I grabbed her around the hips to secure her in place.

Sade threw her free hand in the air and slapped her own ass then froze, dragging her nails across my chest. "Baby, I'm about to cum." She grabbed my wrists. "Baby, I'm about to c-c-cum," she said, bracing herself this time. "HERE IT CUUMMSS," she yelled, happily rolling off me then laying absolutely still.

"Now that shit right there, baby"—I kissed her lips—"that shit right there was the best sex we ever had."

"Y-y-yeah," she responded, still a little shaken. "Maybe you need to spend the night in jail a little more often," she joked.

"That ain't funny," I said in all seriousness.

"Oh, you just need to stop it, Mack." Sade kissed my deflating showstopper. "Oh, what's going on here?" She lifted up ol' flappy. "Why you look so down?" She smiled at it. "You want mommy to make you happy again?"

I shook its head yes, and she went on ahead and made that fallen soldier a master sergeant.

Chapter Three

MACK

I was filling my gas-guzzling black Suburban up with some super unleaded at a Gulf gas station in Elmont, Long Island, and Anton was in my passenger seat, smoking a Philly and bopping his head to one of R. Kelly's cheaters-only anthems.

"I should take this shit to the carwash." I ran my finger across the door. "Every time it rains, I gotta get this shit washed." A horn beeped from behind my truck. I paid no attention to it, until it beeped again.

Anton looked out his window toward the back of the truck. "Be easy," he yelled out. "We almost done."

The horn beeped again, and I walked over to the green Infiniti, ready to knock somebody out. Pineapple-scented fresheners inside the car released a fragrance that clawed at the air when the window rolled down.

I'm a, I'm a, I'm a flirt
Soon as I see her walk up in the club, I'm a flirt

It had Virginia license plates and a decent-sounding stereo. The woman behind the wood-grain looked so good, I almost forgot why I walked over there in the first place. She was brown-skinned with chinky eyes and high cheekbones. Her lips were thin and coated with earth-toned gloss. She wore her hair cut short but straight, a couple of spikes toward the side of her head.

She turned her music down. "Well, what you want, playa?"

Winkin' eyes at me when I roll up on them dubs I'm
a flirt
Sometimes when I'm with my chick on the low, I'm
a flirt

"Why you keep beeping that horn behind us? You see how big that truck is? It takes a minute to fill up, you know."

"I got an appointment to get to. Traffic is going to be straight bananas on the Cross Island." She looked over at the traffic under the crosswalk.

"You'll make it. My shit should just about be filled."

I walked to the pump and pulled the hose out my gas tank. "You could've said the shit was finished," I said, looking at Anton as I activated the auto-start. I pulled over some then walked back to her after she got out to pump her gas. "Hey, I'm sorry about that earlier." I extended my hand. "I thought you was some dick trying to be a smart ass. My name's Mack."

"No, it was just li'l ol' me." She smiled and bent over to pick up the gas card she'd dropped.

And when she's wit' her man looking at me, damn right, I'm a flirt
So, homie, don't bring your girl to me to meet, 'cause I'm a flirt
And, baby, don't bring your girlfriend to eat, 'cause I'm a flirt

Looking at her in the car, it was hard tell to that her legs were so thick, but she was firm and muscular, like really stacking, *mayne.* "So what's your name, love?" I looked down at my watch. I'd almost forgotten that we had somewhere to be too.

"Joi," she said, keeping an eye on the price of the gas tank. She placed the nozzle back in the holder and stood in front of me, her arms folded.

"Anyway, I do promotions at Club Phenomenon, down Rockaway Boulevard. I thought maybe one day you and some of your girlfriends could come through and show some love. We could always use a new face up in there, a fresh, fine face such as yours. First few drinks on me."

She looked at me and laughed. She put the hand down on the hood of her car to support herself from falling over. "You is mad corny, yo. Is that your best line?"

"Naw. My best lines come in li'l baggies about this size." I demonstrated with my fingers.

"Yeah? Well, I'm good on that. What you tryin'-a holla for anyway? You all cute in the face and whatnot, I know you got wifey at home biting her nails down to the cuticle."

"Not even. I won't front though. I do have a lot of friends."

"Friends, huh? So I guess you just want me to be one of your new friends? Homie, lover, friend, fuck buddy?"

> *Please believe it unless your game is tight and you trust her*
> *Then don't bring her 'round me 'cause I'm a flirt*

"Yo, that's not even how I'm coming at you. Them other niggaz got your mind wrong. I just saw a pretty lady and took a chance. Besides, you never know when you may need a friend like me."

"Oh really? Let me ask you something? Do it look like I might be needing a friend's help anytime soon?" Joi chuckled. "Oh, you thought because I'm from VA your New York accent was going to give you some sort of leeway into some drawers? I don't have time for this. I'm out." She opened her car door.

I totally ignored the bullshit Joi was spitting. "You got a man, Joi?"

"Something like that."

"A'ight. So let's cut the small talk. Here goes a flyer and my card. Come on down and have a good time, baby. Promise, you won't regret it." I smiled.

Joi looked at me over her shades for a second then reached down into the cup holder inside her car. "You can call me after seven p.m. during the week. That's when my minutes start." She laughed.

"I hear ya, baby. So that's what's up. I'm-a holla at you real soon."

She stepped inside her car, beeping as she pulled off toward the Cross Island Parkway. Getting inside the truck, I said to Anton, "Now that's how you recruit, boy."

"Anybody could've done that. All you did was give the bitch a flyer. So what that mean? You keep talking about this pimping shit, but I ain't seen shit yet. You be fucking the strippers for free and all, but you not pimping."

"You'll see. Look at me, I am a gorgeous mutha-fucka, and women love that. Don't ever let no bitch tell you that looks don't matter. This is where it's at." I stroked my goatee. "This fly shit right here." I smiled, looking in my rearview, and pushed back my bushy eyebrows. "Personality is for psychologists," I said as I headed down Linden Boulevard.

A white-and-blue Q4 bus stopped at a red light in front of us and released a cloud of smog. "Close the windows," I said, turning on the vent. "This is why I hate coming down this block. I'm taking the back street." I turned left on 227th.

"So what you and Cocaine was talking about?"

"I'll let you know. Don't be opening your mouth about it either when we get to his house. You know how that nigga be getting when dudes start asking about shit he didn't bring up to them himself."

"I ain't worried about his ass. He might've put OPT together, but I'm the cat that be putting in all the work."

Cocaine, founder of OPT, On Point Killers, had more schemes, scams, and smarts than any man I ever knew. OPT was a team of thorough wolves based solely in New York City, known for getting that paper, and stomping in a head or two, if it came down to it. Non-believers became victims of the human pool table effect, eight balls in the corner pockets of our younger shorties-in-training hugging the block as if it were a surrogate father.

Cocaine was forty-six and straight out of an old school called "hard knock life." He was sentenced to ten years in prison when he was sixteen for killing Watty, his mother's boyfriend. Watty was beating the shit out of his mother one night and knocked her through a glass coffee table. Cocaine shot him with a gun he was holding for a friend. According to Cocaine, his mother only respected Watty when he was applying that chokehold around her scrawny little neck. And she only seemed to follow orders when she got a slap across the lips.

Even though it was some fucked-up shit to grow up seeing, it opened son's eyes in understanding a bitch. They wanted a man to be in control, to tell them what to do, and even welcomed a beating, minor or major, if they consciously ever stepped out of line.

All throughout Cocaine's entire life, he ain't never saw any man love his mother. She never asked for respect. She was a poor excuse and a walking embarrassment in his eyes because, after it was really all said and done, it turned out his moms was a prostitute and a dope fiend. It was still etched in his head, the day he came home from school and his moms was fucking and doing dope right on his bed. Now if his own momma wasn't shit and he never felt what it was like to know that kind of love, how in the fuck could anybody ever expect that man to love and respect another woman?

Me and Cocaine met when I did two years of fed time for gun-running. We spent the last two years of his bid exchanging ideas. We got along so good that when I came home he had a spot for me in Queens Village and a lil' Honda Civic at the time. When I was put down with OPT, everything changed.

Cocaine had a stable of bitches working for him, regular bitches with jobs, others just trying to make a dollar. My job was to recruit for him. His clients consisted of average niggaz, white boys from Long Island and the Upper East Side of Manhattan, police, and some anonymous rappers. His biggest clientele was the husbands tired of the same ol' sloppy, aged, wrinkled pussy they was getting after twenty years of marriage and who left their desperate housewives crying their eyes out at home.

A lot of dudes was jealous because I didn't have to go through the initiation process they did. I got in because he knew I could make that dough for him. And if one more of them faggots questioned why I didn't get beat in, they'd be dead.

Cocaine usually didn't have to say anything twice. He had a short fuse. And an even shorter one when it came to his woman, Cakes, an ex-stripper from Michigan that he scooped at a party. She was on the books too. After he'd showed her what kind of bank he was dealing with, she was on the first Greyhound running. She was the epitome of what a dime should look like, 5-9, slender, bronze complexion. Her name was tatted across her chest and was followed by "Cocaine's Property."

She was his main investment, but there was a problem. He beat on her so bad at times that she couldn't always look presentable enough to work. He didn't like no one in the family looking at her unless she was on duty. She was *his* woman.

"Yo!" I knocked on Cocaine's front door. I said to Anton as he got out my truck, "Leave that window cracked so that shit don't be like no oven when we leave." I rapped on the door again. "Yo!"

"Who it is? What it be like?" he said, answering the door in a Rahsaan Ali robe. "Pimping." He smiled. "What's happening, broth?" He widened the door so we could enter.

"You know me. I just be doing what it do," I responded, standing in the patio.

"What's up, Ton? You gonna come in, or you just gonna stand there like a fucking porch monkey?" Cocaine laughed. "Get your ass on in here." He looked up and down the street before closing the door. He said to Anton, "You get my new strippers for the club yet?"

"I'm still working on it. The girl ain't been home. What you want me to do?" Anton shrugged his shoulders.

"Yeah, you absolutely right. What the fuck he gonna do, Mack?" Cocaine shook his head as we walked into the living room. He walked over to the stereo. "Y'all niggaz want something to drink?"

"You got some Grey Goose?" Anton asked.

"Yeah." Cocaine searched for the remote to his stereo. "What you want, Pimping?"

Before I could answer, his phone rang at the same time he found the remote.

"Yeah," he answered. "Look, Trish, you have your ass here before eight tonight. That's it," he said and disconnected the call.

No sooner had he stuck it down in the pocket of his robe than it rang again. He looked down at the caller ID display and frowned. "Looky here, y'all, I gotta take this call upstairs. Make your own drinks. You know where they at." He pressed power on the remote then jogged up the stairs.

The front door unlocked, and in walked Cakes, her hands filled with shopping bags. She was absolutely fucking gorgeous, man. She closed the door with the heel of her foot. "What's good, y'all?" She placed her bags in front of a blue reclining lounge chair next to a four-foot potted bella palm tree, where an automatic sterling silver mini-sprinkler connected to the hose of the bar's sink hose sprayed a misty dew every ten minutes.

Cakes' long, sexy, lotioned ass shined and stretched outside of her poom-poom shorts as she strode across the green living room carpet and placed her bags at the bar. "What y'all doing here?" She looked specifically at me, while pouring herself a drink. "What's up, boo? You looking kind of snazzy today. Where you off to, a job interview?" she sarcastically asked.

"Naw. I'm off to see the 'wizard' about some muthafucking brains, bitch." I grabbed my crotch like Michael Jackson after his acquittal.

Cakes chuckled. "That was actually funny. Anton, you all sitting up there like you don't acknowledge perfection in your presence, nigga. Hail a prominent ho when you see one, nigga." She bounced her ass off his leg.

"Hail the ho, hail the ho." Anton bent over laughing.

"That's right. My shit is magic on the johnson." She winked at me.

"So what you got over there?" Anton joked. "A bag of tricks?"

"Shit you can't afford on the salary you making."

Anton pulled out a roll of hundreds. "My pockets is fine."

"Pennies, nigga. You ain't getting it like Mack. Ain't that right?" Cakes smiled and looked at me.

"I'm not even in this. Y'all two always going at it. Shit, if I didn't know y'all wasn't stupid, I'd think you two was fucking."

"Yeah, me too," Cocaine said, stepping down the last stair and into the end of the conversation. "But I know that ain't the case, right, y'all? Because there's a rule about fucking the help." He snatched Cakes' bags off the floor and threw them on the couch.

"Hi, daddy. I missed you." Cakes kissed his lips.

Cocaine turned his head and pushed her away. "You must be out of your mind, girl. What, you planning on going out on a date somewhere? What the fuck is all this bullshit, Cakes?" Then he started tossing shit out the bags onto the floor.

"I told you I was going shopping earlier. I can't be wearing repeat outfits when the work come in. I'm not like them other raggedy bitches you got munching and punching the clock, daddy. You know my style—Gots to look good for the customers."

As Cakes bent over to collect the fallen luxury items, Cocaine kicked her square in the ass. I could've sworn I saw a pound of that lotion on her shiny legs jump off her skin. She fell onto the pile of clothing in front of her and quickly turned over.

Cocaine never liked anyone talking slick, especially no high-priced, hooker-ass ho. Especially when he was feeding and clothing them.

A tear rushed down her eye. "What the hell is you doing?"

"Get this damn shit off my living room floor, Cakes. You spent all of your allowance money on this bullshit. Get the fuck up to your room. NOW!"

Cakes quickly scrambled to her feet and stuffed all the clothing back into the bags. Then she slowly walked up the stairs, rubbing her ass.

Anton and me looked at each other then looked at him.

"What?" Cocaine asked in a tone similar to Raphael Saadiq. "When the day comes I let one of my hoes talk to me like that, it'll be a rainy day in Southern California, you hear that? You give 'em one inch and they'll have you living in your own yard under the fucking gas meter." He sipped his drink. "Y'all muthafuckas know what I'm saying to you? Mack, you the next nigga up. I hope you paying attention. I'm trying to train your ass. You got potential, boy. Don't go letting me down."

Cocaine poured two shots of tequila, one for Anton, one for me. "Y'all niggaz, have a drink with me." He held up his glass.

Anton told him, "You hard on these hoes, man."

"What, nigga? You need to be following in this man's footsteps." Cocaine pointed to me. "This fool is a pussy magnet. He bring the bitches into work."

Anton was upset. "And I don't?"

"You couldn't bring in the New Year without

tripping over last month." Cocaine laughed. "You used to be on point. You slipping."

"What you mean, man? How much money and bitches I brought in last year?"

"That's not the point. It's all about chutes and ladders, baby."

Every now and again, when Cocaine had a little drink in his system, he'd just start making up some mind-boggling-ass phrase then build on it. Sometimes it'd make perfect sense; other times it sounded just as crazy as Gnarls Barkley singing the movie soundtrack for *One Flew over the Cuckoo's Nest*.

Anton asked, "What you mean, *chutes and ladders*?"

"Chutes and ladders, nigga." Cocaine coughed after inhaling deeply. "Rewards and consequences. You always start out on a good path, collecting points, respect, street cred and shit like that—That be the ladders that help you climb to the top of this game. Then you got them chutes—bitch-ass niggaz, snitches, informants, and haters. Shit of that nature is the chutes that'll land your ass in a world of consequences. The chutes is the shit that'll make you fall, and it won't have shit to do with autumn. The whole idea of this pimp shit is to keep climbing the ladder until all the muthafuckas under you look like ants. This pimp shit be about the constant climb. The trick is to never look down, especially if you afraid of heights, muthafucka, because it's just not about pimping these hoes, it's about pimping the system. You ever lose focus of that, and you'll just be part of some bitch's photographic memory." He released a cloud of London fog.

"So what you saying, man?"

"I'm saying I see your true colors shining through, Ton."

"Yo, y'all is bugging," I said. "I got shit to do, Coke. You straight with that paper." I stood up.

Lately Cocaine had been stressing Anton about his inability to make things happen as he used to. He'd been that way ever since Anton had popped these two auxiliary police officers in Flushing Meadows, Queens a couple of months back. I felt in my gut that Cocaine wanted Ton dead, because his mouth would leak if he ever was caught by the pigs for that murder.

"Yeah, youngblood. We be done. Y'all seen my brother around? I ain't heard from him in a couple of days."

"Naw, man, not me," I said. "I just got out."

He said to Ton, "You, nigga?"

"I ain't seen him in a couple of days."

"All right, whatever. Hit my phone later, Mack," Cocaine said as we walked out the door. "We need to talk."